Also by Alice Elliott Dark

Naked to the Waist

Alice Elliott Dark

In the Gloaming

STORIES

SIMON & SCHUSTER

SIMON & SCHUSTER
Rockefeller Center
1230 Avenue of the Americas
New York, NY 10020

Simon & Schuster and colophon are registered trademarks
of Simon & Schuster, Inc.

Designed by Jeanette Olender
Manufactured in the United States of America

1   3   5   7   9   10   8   6   4   2

Library of Congress Cataloging-in-Publication Data
Dark, Alice Elliott.
In the gloaming: stories / Alice Elliott Dark.
p. cm.
1. Pennsylvania—Social life and customs—Fiction.
2. City and town life—Pennsylvania—Fiction.   I. Title.
PS3554.A714I52   2000
813'.54—dc21   99-27542   CIP
ISBN 0-684-86521-1

"In the Gloaming" previously appeared in *The New Yorker*.
"Triage" and "Home" previously appeared in *DoubleTake*.
"The Tower" previously appeared in *Book*.
"The Secret Spot" previously appeared in *Redbook*.
"Maniacs" previously appeared in *Five Points*.
"Watch the Animals" previously appeared in *Harper's*.

thanks, thanks, thanks

Denise Roy, David Rosenthal,
Brenda Copeland; Henry Dunow; Larry Dark;
Linda Asher, Susan Ketchin, Katrina Kenison;
Mona Simpson; Craig Musser;
the National Endowment for the Arts.

for

Alice Dixon, Francie Rentschler,
and Polly Mackie—
unconditional inspirations

Contents

In the Gloaming, 11

Dreadful Language, 41

The Jungle Lodge, 77

Triage, 107

The Tower, 117

The Secret Spot, 143

Close, 171

Maniacs, 197

Home, 235

Watch the Animals, 269

In the Gloaming

HE WANTED to talk again, suddenly. During the days, he still brooded, scowling at the swimming pool from the vantage point of his wheelchair, where he sat covered with blankets in spite of the summer heat. In the evenings, though, he became more like his old self: his *old* old self, really. He became sweeter, the way he'd been as a child, before he began to gird himself with layers of irony and clever remarks. He spoke with an openness that astonished her. No one she knew talked that way— no man at least. After he was asleep, Janet would run through the conversations in her mind and realize what it was she wished she'd said. She knew she was generally considered sincere, but that had more to do with her being a good listener than with how she expressed herself. She found it hard work to keep up with him, but it was the work she had pined for all her life.

A month earlier, after a particularly long and grueling visit with a friend who'd taken the train down to Wynnemoor from New York, Laird had declared a new policy: no visitors, no telephone calls. She didn't blame him. People who hadn't seen him for a while were often shocked to tears by his appearance, and rather than having them cheer him up, he felt obliged to comfort *them*. She'd overheard bits of some of those conversations. The final one was no worse than others, but Laird was fed up. He'd said more than once that he wasn't cut out to be the brave one, the one who would inspire everybody to walk away from a visit with him feeling uplifted, shaking their heads in wonder. He had liked being the most handsome and missed it very much. When he'd had enough he went into a self-imposed retreat, complete with a wall of silence and other ascetic practices that kept him busy for several weeks.

Then he softened. Not only did he want to talk again; he wanted to talk to *her*.

It began the night they ate outside on the terrace for the first time all summer. Afterward, Martin—her husband—got up to make a telephone call, but Janet stayed in her wicker chair, resting before clearing the table. It was one of those moments when she felt nostalgic for cigarettes. On nights like this, when the air was completely still, she used to blow her famous smoke rings for the children, dutifully obeying their commands to blow one through another or three in a row, or to make big, ropey circles that expanded as they floated up to the heavens. She did exactly what they wanted, for as long as they wanted, sometimes going through a quarter of a pack before they allowed her to stop. Incredibly, neither Anne nor Laird became smokers. Just the opposite; they nagged at her to quit and were pleased when she finally did. She wished they had been just a little bit sorry. It was a part of their childhood coming to an end, after all.

Out of habit, she took note of the first lightning bug, the first star. The lawn darkened, and the flowers that had sulked in the heat all day suddenly released their perfumes. She laid her head back on the rim of the chair and closed her eyes. Soon she was following Laird's breathing and found herself picking up the vital rhythms, breathing along. It was so peaceful, being near him like this. How many mothers spend so much time with their thirty-three-year-old sons? She had as much of him now as she'd had when he was an infant—more, because she had the memory of the intervening years as well, to round out her thoughts about him. When they sat quietly together she felt as close to him as she ever had. It was still him in there, inside the failing shell. *She still enjoyed him.*

"The gloaming," he said, suddenly.

She nodded dreamily, automatically, then sat up. She turned to him. "What?" Although she'd heard.

"I remember when I was little you took me over to the picture window and told me that in Scotland this time of day was called the 'gloaming.'"

Her skin tingled. She cleared her throat, quietly, taking care not to make too much of the event that he was talking again. "You thought I said it was 'gloomy.'"

He gave a smile, then looked at her searchingly. "I always thought it hurt you somehow that the day was over, but you said it was a beautiful time because for a few moments the purple light made the whole world look like the Scottish highlands on a summer night."

"Yes. As if all the earth was covered with heather."

"I'm sorry I never saw Scotland," he said.

"You're a Scottish lad nonetheless—at least on my side." She remembered offering to take him to Scotland once, but Laird hadn't been interested. By then, he was in college and already sure of his own destinations, which had diverged so thoroughly from hers. "I'm amazed you remember that conversation. You couldn't have been more than seven."

"I've been remembering a lot, lately."

"Have you?"

"Mostly about when I was very small. I suppose it comes from having you take care of me again. Sometimes, when I wake up and see your face, I feel I can remember you looking in on me when I was in my crib. I remember your dresses."

"Oh no!" She laughed lightly.

"You always had the loveliest expression," he said.

She was astonished, caught off-guard. Then, she had a memory, too—of her leaning over Laird's crib and suddenly having a picture of looking up at her own mother. "I know what you mean," she said.

"You do, don't you?"

He regarded her in a close, intimate way that made her self-conscious. She caught herself swinging her leg nervously, like a pendulum, and stopped.

"Mom," he said. "There are still a few things I need to do. I have to write a will, for one thing."

Her heart went flat. In his presence she always maintained that he would get well. She wasn't sure she could discuss the other possibility.

"Thank you," he said.

"For what?"

"For not saying that there's plenty of time for that, or some similar sentiment."

"The only reason I didn't say it was to avoid the cliché, not because I don't believe it."

"You believe there is plenty of time?"

She hesitated; he noticed and leaned forward slightly. "I believe there is time," she said.

"Even if I were healthy, it would be a good idea."

"I suppose."

"I don't want to leave it until it's too late. You wouldn't want me to suddenly leave everything to the nurses, would you?"

She laughed, pleased to hear him joking again. "All right, all right, I'll call the lawyer."

"That would be great." There was a pause. "Is this still your favorite time of day, Mom?"

"Yes, I suppose it is," she said, "although I don't think in terms of favorites anymore."

"Never mind favorites, then. What else do you like?"

"What do you mean?" she asked.

"I mean exactly that."

"I don't know. I care about all the ordinary things. You know what I like."

"Name one thing."

"I feel silly."

"Please?"

"All right. I like my patch of lilies of the valley, under the trees over there. Now can we change the subject?"

"Name one more thing."

"Why?"

"I want to get to know you."

"Oh, Laird, there's nothing to know."

"I don't believe that for a minute."

"But it's true. I'm average. The only extraordinary thing about me is my children."

"All right," he said. "Then let's talk about how you feel about *me.*"

"Do you flirt with your nurses like this when I'm not around?"

"I don't dare. They've got me where they want me." He looked at her. "You're changing the subject."

She smoothed her skirt. "I know how you feel about church, but if you need to talk, I'm sure the minister would be glad to come over. Or if you would rather a doctor . . ."

He laughed.

"What?"

"That you still call psychiatrists 'doctors.' "

She shrugged.

"I don't need a professional, Ma." He laced his hands and pulled at them as he struggled for words.

"What can I do?" she asked.

He met her gaze. "You're where I come from. I need to know about you."

That night she lay awake, trying to think of how she could help, of what, aside from time, she had to offer. She couldn't imagine.

She was anxious the next day when he was sullen again, but the next night, and on each succeeding night, the dusk worked its spell. She set dinner on the table outside, and afterward, when Martin had vanished into the maw of his study, she and Laird began to speak. The air around them seemed to crackle with the energy they were creating in their effort to know and be known. Were other people so close, she wondered? She never had been, not to anybody. Certainly she and Martin had never really connected, not soul to soul, and with her friends, no matter how loyal and reliable, she always had a sense of what she could do that would alienate them. Of course, her friends had the option of cutting her off, and Martin could always ask for a divorce, whereas Laird was a captive audience. Parents and children were all captive audiences to each other; in view of this, it was amazing how little comprehension there was of one another's story. Everyone stopped paying attention so early on, thinking they had figured it all out.

She recognized that she was as guilty of this as anyone. She was still surprised whenever she went over to her daughter Anne's house and saw how neat she was. In her mind, Anne was still a sloppy teenager who threw sweaters into the corner of her closet and candy wrappers under her bed. It still surprised her that Laird wasn't interested in girls. He had been, hadn't he? She remembered lying awake listening for him to come home, hoping that he was smart enough to apply what he knew about the facts of life, to take precautions.

Now she had the chance to let go of these old notions. It wasn't that she liked everything about Laird— there was much that remained foreign to her—but she wanted to know about all of it. As she came to her senses every morning in the moment or two after she awoke, she found herself aching with love and gratitude, as if he were a small perfect creature again and she could look forward to a day of watching him grow. She became greedy for their evenings and replaced her daily, half-facetious, half-hopeful reading of the horoscope with a new habit of tracking the time the sun would set. As the summer waned, she drew satisfaction from seeing it listed as earlier and earlier—it meant she didn't have to wait as long.

She took to sleeping late, shortening the day even further. It was ridiculous, she knew. She was behaving like a girl with a crush, behaving absurdly. It was a feeling she thought she'd never have again, and now here it was. She immersed herself in it, living her life for the twilight moment when his eyes would begin to glow, the signal that he was stirring into consciousness. Then her real day would begin.

"Dad ran off quickly," he said one night.

She'd been wondering if he noticed it.

"He had a phone call to make," she said automatically.

Laird looked directly into her eyes, his expression one of gentle reproach. He was letting her know he had caught her in the central lie of her life, which was that she understood Martin's obsession with his work. She averted her gaze. The truth was that she had never understood. Why couldn't he sit with her for half an hour after dinner, or if not with her, why not with his dying son?

She turned sharply to look at Laird. The word "dying" had sounded so loudly in her mind that she wondered if she had spoken it, but he showed no reaction. She wished she hadn't even thought it. She tried to stick to good thoughts in his presence. When she couldn't, and he had a bad night afterward, she blamed herself, as her memory efficiently dredged up all the books and magazine articles she had read emphasizing the effect of psychological factors on the course of the disease. She didn't entirely believe it, but she felt compelled to give the benefit of the doubt to every theory that might help. It couldn't do any harm to think positively. And if it gave him a few more months . . .

"I don't think Dad can stand to be around me."

"That's not true." It was true.

"Poor Dad. He's always been a hypochondriac—we have that in common. He must hate this."

"He just wants you to get well."

"If that's what he wants, I'm afraid I'm going to disappoint him. At least this will be the last time I let him down."

He said this merrily, with the old, familiar light darting from his eyes. She allowed herself to be amused. He'd always been fond of teasing and held no subject sacred. As the de facto authority figure in the house—Martin hadn't been home enough to be the real disciplinarian—she'd often been forced to reprimand Laird but, in truth, she shared his sense of humor. She responded to it now by leaning over to cuff him on the arm. It was an automatic gesture, prompted by a burst of high spirits that took no notice of the circumstances. It was a mistake. Even through the thickness of his terry cloth robe, her knuckles knocked on bone. There was nothing left of him.

"It's his loss," she said, the shock of Laird's thinness making her serious again. It was the furthest she would go in criticizing Martin. She'd always felt it her duty to maintain a benign image of him for the children. He'd become a character of her invention, with a whole range of postulated emotions whereby he missed them when he was away on a business trip and thought of them every few minutes when he had to work late.

Some years earlier, when she was secretly seeing a

doctor—a psychiatrist—she had finally admitted to herself that Martin was never going to be the lover she had dreamed of. He was an ambitious, competitive, self-absorbed man who probably should never have gotten married. It was such a relief to be able to face it that she had wanted to share the news with her children, only to discover that they were dependent on the myth. They could hate his work, but they could not bring themselves to believe he had any choice in the matter. She decided to leave them to their own discoveries.

"Thank you, Ma. It's his loss in your case, too."

A throbbing began behind her eyes, angering her. The last thing she wanted to do was cry—there would be plenty of time for that. "It's not all his fault," she said when she had regained some measure of control. "I'm not very good at talking about myself. I was brought up not to."

"So was I," he said.

"Yes, I suppose you were."

"Luckily, I didn't pay any attention." He grinned.

"I hope not," she said—and meant it. "Can I get you anything?"

"A new immune system?"

She frowned, trying to disguise the way his joke had touched on her prayers. "Very funny. I was thinking more along the lines of an iced tea or an extra blanket."

"I'm fine. I'm getting tired, actually."

Her entire body went on the alert, and she searched his face anxiously for signs of deterioration. Her nerves darted and pricked whenever he wanted anything—her adrenaline rushed. The fight-or-flight response, she supposed. She had often wanted to flee, but had forced herself to stay, to fight with what few weapons she had. She responded to his needs, making sure there was a fresh, clean set of sheets ready when he was tired, food for his hunger. It was what she could do.

"Shall I get the nurse?" She pushed her chair back from the table.

"Okay," Laird said weakly. He stretched out his hand to her, and the incipient moonlight illuminated his skin so it shone like alabaster. His face had turned ashy. It was a sight that made her stomach drop. She ran for Maggie, and by the time they returned Laird's eyes were closed, his head lolling to one side. Automatically, Janet looked for a stirring in his chest. There it was; his shoulders expanded; he still breathed. Always, in the second before she saw movement, she became cold and clinical as she braced herself for the possibility of discovering that he was dead.

Maggie had her fingers on his wrist and was counting his pulse against the second hand on her watch, her lips moving. She laid his limp hand back on his lap. "Fast," she pronounced.

"I'm not surprised," Janet said, masking her fear with authority. "We had a long talk."

Maggie frowned. "Now I'll have to wake him up again for his meds."

"Yes, I suppose that's true. I forgot about that."

Janet wheeled him into his makeshift room downstairs and helped Maggie lift him into the rented hospital bed. Although he weighed almost nothing, it was
really a job for two; his weight was dead weight. In front
of Maggie, she was all brusque efficiency, except for the
moment when her fingers strayed to touch Laird's pale
cheek and she prayed she hadn't done any harm.

"Who's your favorite author?" he asked one night.

"Oh, there are so many," she said.

"Your real favorite."

She thought. "The truth is there are certain subjects
I find attractive more than certain authors. I seem to
read in cycles, to fulfill emotional yearnings."

"Such as?"

"Books about people who go off to live in Africa or
Australia or the South Seas."

He laughed. "That's fairly self-explanatory. What
else?"

"When I really hate life I enjoy books about real mur-
ders. 'True crime,' I think they're called now. They're
very punishing."

"Is that what's so compelling about them? I could
never figure it out. I just knew that at certain times I
loved the gore, even though I felt absolutely disgusted
with myself for being interested in it."

"You need to think about when those times were.
That will tell you a lot." She paused. "I don't like reading about sex."

"Big surprise!"

"No, no," she said. "It's not for the reason you think, or not only for that reason. You see me as a prude, I know, but remember, it's part of a mother's job to come across that way. Although perhaps I went a bit far . . ."

He shrugged amiably. "Water under the bridge. But go on about sex."

"I think it should be private. I always feel as though these writers are showing off when they describe a sex scene. They're not really trying to describe sex, but to demonstrate that they're not afraid to write about it. As if they're thumbing noses at their mothers."

He made a moue.

Janet went on. "You don't think there's an element of that? I *do* question their motives, because I don't think sex can ever be accurately portrayed. The sensations and the emotions are—beyond language. If you only describe the mechanics, the effect is either clinical or pornographic, and if you try to describe intimacy instead, you wind up with abstractions. The only sex you could describe fairly well is bad sex—and who wants to read about that, for God's sake, when everyone is having bad sex of their own?"

"Mother!" He was laughing helplessly, his arms hanging limply over the sides of his chair.

"I mean it. To me it's like reading about someone using the bathroom."

"Good grief!"

"Now who's the prude?"

"I never said I wasn't," he said. "Maybe we should change the subject."

She looked out across the land. The lights were on in other people's houses, giving the evening the look of early fall. The leaves were different, too, becoming droopy. The grass was dry, even with all the watering and tending by the gardener. The summer was nearly over.

"Maybe we shouldn't," she said. "I've been wondering. Was that side of life satisfying for you?"

"Ma, tell me you're not asking me about my sex life."

She took her napkin and folded it carefully, lining up the edges and running her fingers along the hems. She felt very calm, very pulled together and all of a piece, as if she'd finally got the knack of being a dignified woman. She threaded her fingers and lay her hands in her lap. "I'm asking about your love life," she said. "Did you love, and were you loved in return?"

"Yes."

"I'm glad."

"That was easy," he said.

"Oh, I've gotten very easy, in my old age."

"Does Dad know about this?" His eyes were twinkling wickedly.

"Don't be fresh," she said.

"You started it."

"Then I'm stopping it. Now."

He made a funny face, and then another, until she could no longer keep from smiling. His routine carried her back to memories of his childhood efforts to charm her: watercolors of her favorite vistas (unrecognizable without the captions), bouquets of violets self-consciously flung into her lap, a chore performed without prompting. He had always gone too far, then backtracked to regain even footing. She had always allowed herself to be wooed.

Suddenly she realized—Laird was the love of her life.

One night it rained hard. She decided to serve the meal in the kitchen, as Martin was out. They ate in silence; she was freed from the compulsion to keep up the steady stream of chatter that she used to affect when Laird hadn't talked at all; now she knew she could save her words for afterward. He ate nothing but comfort foods lately—mashed potatoes, vanilla ice cream, rice pudding. The days of his strict macrobiotic regime, and all the cooking classes she had taken in order to help him along with it, were long past. His body was essentially a thing of the past, too; when he ate, he was feeding what was left of his mind. He seemed to want to recapture the cosseted feeling he'd had when he was sick as a child and she would serve him flat ginger ale, and toast soaked in cream, and play endless card games with him, using his blanket-covered legs as a table. In those days, too, there'd been a general sense of giving way to illness: then, he let himself go completely because he knew he would soon be better and active and have a million things expected of him again. Now he let himself go because he had fought long enough.

Finally, he pushed his bowl toward the middle of the table, signaling that he was finished. (His table manners had gone to pieces. Who cared?) She felt a light, jittery excitement, the same jazzy feeling she got when she was in a plane that was just picking up speed on the runway. She arranged her fork and knife on the rim of her plate and pulled her chair in closer. "I had an odd dream last night," she said.

His eyes remained dull.

She waited uncertainly, thinking that perhaps she had started to talk too soon. "Would you like something else to eat?"

He shook his head. There was no will in his expression. His refusal was purely physical, a gesture coming from the satiation in his stomach. An animal walking away from its bowl, she thought.

To pass the time, she carried the dishes to the sink, gave them a good, hot rinse, and put them in the dishwasher. She carried the ice cream to the counter, pulled a spoon from the drawer, and scraped together a mouthful of the thick, creamy residue that stuck to the inside of the lid. She ate it without thinking, so the sudden sweetness caught her by surprise. All the while she kept track of Laird, but every time she thought she noticed signs of his readiness to talk and hurried back to the table, she found his face still blank.

She went to the window. The lawn had become a floodplain and was filled with broad pools. The branches of the evergreens sagged, and the sky was the same uniform grayish yellow it had been since morning. She saw him focus his gaze on the line where the treetops touched the heavens, and she understood. There was no lovely interlude on this rainy night, no heathered dusk. The gray landscape had taken the light out of him.

"I'm sorry," she said aloud, as if it were her fault.

He gave a tiny, helpless shrug.

She hovered for a few moments, hoping; but his face was slack, and she gave up. She felt utterly forsaken, too disappointed and agitated to sit with him and watch the rain. "It's all right," she said. "It's a good night to watch television."

She wheeled him to the den and left him with Maggie, then did not know what to do with herself. She had no contingency plan for this time. It was usually the one period of the day when she did not need the anesthesia of tennis games, bridge lessons, volunteer work, errands. She had not considered the present possibility. For some time, she hadn't given any thought to what Martin would call "the big picture." Her conversations with Laird had lulled her into inventing a parallel big picture of her own. She realized that a part of her had worked out a whole scenario: the summer evenings would blend into fall; then, gradually, the winter would arrive, heralding chats by the fire, Laird resting his feet on the pigskin ottoman in the den while she dutifully knitted her yearly Christmas sweaters for Anne's children.

She had allowed herself to imagine a future. That had been her mistake. This silent, endless evening was her punishment, a reminder of how things really were.

She did not know where to go in her own house and ended up wandering through the rooms, propelled by a vague, hunted feeling. Several times she turned around, expecting someone to be there but, of course, no one ever was; she was quite alone. Eventually she realized she was imagining a person in order to give material properties to the source of her wounds. She was inventing a villain.

There should be a villain, shouldn't there? There should be an enemy, a devil, an evil force that could be driven out. Her imagination had provided it with aspects of a corporeal presence so she could pretend, for a moment, that there was a real enemy hovering around her, someone she could have the police come and take away. But the enemy was part of Laird, and neither he nor she nor any of the doctors or experts or ministers could separate the two.

She went upstairs and took a shower. She barely paid attention to her own body anymore and only noticed abstractly that the water was too hot, her skin turning pink. Afterward, she sat on the chaise longue in her bedroom and tried to read. She heard something; she leaned forward and cocked her head toward the sound.

Was that Laird's voice? Suddenly she believed that he had begun to talk after all—she believed he was talking to Maggie. She dressed and rushed downstairs. He was alone in the den, alone with the television. He didn't hear or see her. She watched him take a drink from a cup, his hand shaking badly. It was a plastic cup with a straw poking through the lid, the kind used by small children while they are learning to drink. It was supposed to prevent accidents, but it couldn't stop his hands from trembling. He managed to spill the juice anyway.

Laird had always coveted the decadent pile of cashmere lap blankets she had collected over the years in the duty-free shops of the various British airports. Now, in spite of the mild weather, he wore one around his shoulders when they sat outside and spread another over his knees. She remembered similar balmy nights when he would arrive home from soccer practice after dark, a towel slung around his neck.

"I suppose it has to be in the church," he said.

"I think it should," she said, "but it's up to you."

"I guess it's not the most timely moment to make a statement about my personal disbeliefs. But I'd like you to keep it from being too lugubrious. No lilies, for instance."

"God forbid."

"And have some decent music."

"Such as?"

"I had an idea, but now I can't remember."

He pressed his hands to his eyes. His fingers were so transparent that they looked as if he were holding them over a flashlight.

"Please buy a smashing dress, something mournful yet elegant."

"All right."

"And don't wait until the last minute."

She didn't reply.

Janet gave up on the idea of a rapprochement between Martin and Laird; she felt freer when she stopped hoping for it. Martin rarely came home for dinner anymore. Perhaps he was having an affair? It was a thought she'd never allowed herself to have before, but it didn't threaten her now. Good for him, she even decided, in her strongest, most magnanimous moments. Good for him if he's actually feeling bad and trying to do something to make himself feel better.

Anne was brave and chipper during her visits, yet when she walked back out to her car, she would wrap her arms around her ribs and shudder. "I don't know how you do it, Mom. Are you really all right?" she'd ask, with genuine concern.

"Anne's become such a hopeless matron," Laird always said, with fond exasperation, when he and his mother were alone again later. Once, Janet began to tease him for finally coming to friendly terms with his sister, but she cut it short when she saw that he was blinking furiously.

They were exactly the children she had hoped to have: a companionable girl, a mischievous boy. It gave her great pleasure to see them together. She did not try to listen to their conversations but watched from a distance, usually from the kitchen as she prepared them a snack reminiscent of their childhood, like watermelon boats or lemonade. Then she would walk Anne to the car, their similar good shoes clacking across the gravel. They hugged, pressing each other's arms, and their brief embraces buoyed them up—forbearance and strength passing back and forth between them like a piece of shared clothing, designated for use by whoever needed it most. It was the kind of moment toward which she had aimed her whole life, a graceful, secure parting at the close of a peaceful afternoon.

After Anne left, Janet always felt a tranquil sensation as she walked back to the house through the humid September air. Everything was so still. Occasionally there were the hums and clicks of a lawnmower or the shrieks of a band of children heading home from school. There were the insects and the birds. It was a straightforward, simple life. She'd tried never to ask for too much, and always to be of use. Simplicity had been her hedge against bad luck. It had worked for so long. For a brief moment, as she stepped lightly up the single slate stair and through the door, her legs still harboring all their former vitality, she could pretend her luck was still holding.

Then she would glance out the window and there

would be the heart-catching sight of Laird, who would never again drop by for a casual visit. Her chest would ache and flutter, a cave full of bats.

Perhaps she'd asked for too much, after all.

"What did you want to be when you grew up?" Laird asked.

"I was expected to be a wife and mother. I accepted that. I wasn't a rebel."

"There must have been something else."

"No," she said. "Oh, I guess I had all the usual fantasies of the day, of being the next Amelia Earhart or Margaret Mead, but that was all they were—fantasies. I wasn't even close to being brave enough. Can you imagine me flying across the ocean on my own?"

She laughed and looked over for his laughter, but he'd fallen asleep.

A friend of Laird's had somehow gotten the mistaken information that Laird had died, so she and Martin received a condolence letter. There was a story about a time a few years back when the friend was with Laird on a bus in New York. They'd been sitting behind two older women, waitresses who began to discuss their income taxes, trying to decide how little of their tip income they could realistically declare without attracting an audit. Each offered up bits of folk wisdom on the subject, describing in detail her particular situation. During a lull in the conversation, Laird stood up.

"Excuse me, I couldn't help but overhear," he said, leaning over them. "May I have your names and addresses, please? I work for the I.R.S."

The entire bus fell silent as everyone watched to see what would happen next. Laird took a small notebook and pen from the inside pocket of his jacket. He faced his captive audience. "I'm part of a new I.R.S. outreach program," he told the group. "For the next ten minutes I'll be taking confessions. Does anyone have anything he or she wants to tell me?"

Smiles. Soon the whole bus was talking, comparing notes—on when they'd first realized he was kidding, on how scared they'd been before they caught on. It was difficult to believe these were the same New Yorkers who were supposed to be so gruff and isolated.

"Laird was the most vital, funniest person I ever met," his friend wrote.

Now, in his wheelchair, he faced off against slow-moving flies, waving them away.

"The gloaming," Laird said.

Janet looked up from her knitting, startled. It was midafternoon, and the living room was filled with bright October sun. "Soon," she said.

He furrowed his brow. A little flash of confusion passed through his eyes, and she realized that for him it was already dark.

He tried to straighten his shawl, his hands shaking. She jumped up to help. Then, when he pointed to the fireplace, she quickly laid the logs as she wondered what was wrong. Was he dehydrated? She thought she recalled that a dimming of the vision was a sign of dehydration. She tried to remember what else she'd read or heard, but even as she grasped for information, facts, her instincts kept interrupting with a deeper, more dreadful thought that vibrated through her, rattling her and making her gasp as she often did when remembering her mistakes, things she wished she hadn't said or done, wished she had the chance to do over. She knew what was wrong, and yet she kept turning away from the truth, her mind spinning in every other possible direction as she worked on the fire, only vaguely noticing how wildly she made the sparks fly as she pumped the old bellows.

Her work was mechanical—she'd made hundreds of fires—and soon there was nothing left to do. She put the screen up and pushed him close, then leaned over to pull his flannel pajamas down to meet his socks, protecting his bare shins. The sun streamed in around him, making him appear trapped between bars of light. She resumed her knitting, with mechanical hands.

"The gloaming," he said again. It did sound somewhat like "gloomy," because his speech was slurred.

"When all the world is purple," she said, hearing herself sound falsely bright. She wasn't sure whether he wanted her to talk. It was some time since he'd spoken much—not long, really, in other people's lives, perhaps two weeks—but she had gone on with their conversations, gradually expanding into the silence until she was telling him stories and he was listening. Sometimes, when his eyes closed, she trailed off and began to drift. There would be a pause that she didn't always realize she was making, but if it went on too long he would call out "Mom?" with an edge of panic in his voice, as if he were waking from a nightmare. Then she would resume, trying to create a seamless bridge between what she'd been thinking and where she had left off.

"It was really your grandfather who gave me my love for the gloaming," she said. "Do you remember him talking about it?"

She looked up politely, expectantly, as if Laird might offer her a conversational reply. He seemed to like hearing the sound of her voice so she went on, her needles clicking. Afterward, she could never remember for sure at what point she'd stopped talking and had floated off into a jumble of her own thoughts, afraid to move, afraid to look up, afraid to know at which exact moment she became alone. All she knew was that at a certain point the fire was in danger of dying out entirely, and when she got up to stir the embers she glanced at him in spite of herself and saw that his fingers were making knitting motions over his chest, the way people did as they were dying. She knew that if she went to get the nurse, Laird would be gone by the time she returned, so she went and stood behind him, leaning over to press her face against his, sliding her hands down his busy arms, helping him along with his fretful stitches until he finished this last piece of work.

Later, after the most pressing calls had been made and Laird's body had been taken away, Janet went up to his old room and lay down on one of the twin beds. She had changed the room into a guest room when he went off to college, replacing his things with guest-room decor, thoughtful touches such as luggage racks at the foot of each bed, a writing desk stocked with paper and pens, heavy wooden hangers, and shoe trees. She made an effort to remember the room as it had been when he was a little boy; she'd chosen a train motif, then had to redecorate when Laird decided trains were silly. He'd wanted it to look like Africa, so she had hired an art student to paint a jungle mural on the walls. When he decided *that* was silly, he hadn't bothered her to do anything about it, but had simply marked time until he could move on.

Anne came over, offered to stay, but was relieved to be sent home to her children.

Presently, Martin came in. Janet was watching the trees turn to mere silhouettes against the darkening sky, fighting the urge to pick up a true-crime book, a debased urge. He lay down on the other bed.

"I'm sorry," he said.

"It's so wrong," she said angrily. She hadn't felt angry until that moment; she had saved it up for him. "A child shouldn't die before his parents. A young man shouldn't spend his early thirties wasting away talking to his mother. He should be out in the world. He shouldn't be thinking about me, or what I care about, or my opinions. He shouldn't have had to return my love to me—it was his to squander. Now I have it all back and I don't know what I'm supposed to do with it," she said.

She could hear Martin weeping in the darkness. He sobbed, and her anger veered away.

They were quiet for some time.

"Is there going to be a funeral?" Martin asked finally.

"Yes. We should start making the arrangements."

"I suppose he told you what he wanted."

"In general. He couldn't decide about the music."

She heard Martin roll onto his side, so that he was facing her across the narrow chasm between the beds. He was still in his office clothes. "I remember being very moved by the bagpipes at your father's funeral."

It was an awkward offering, to be sure, awkward and late, and seemed to come from someone on the periphery of her life who knew her only slightly. It didn't matter; it was perfectly right. Her heart rushed toward it.

"I think Laird would have liked that idea very much," she said.

It was the last moment of the gloaming, the last moment of the day her son died. In a breath, it would be night; the moon hovered behind the trees, already rising to claim the sky, and she told herself she might as well get on with it. She sat up and was running her toes across the bare floor, searching for her shoes, when Martin spoke again, in a tone she used to hear on those long-ago nights when he rarely got home until after the children were in bed and he relied on her to fill him in on what they'd done that day. It was the same curious, shy, deferential tone that had always made her feel as though all the frustrations and boredom and mistakes and rushes of feeling in her days as a mother did indeed add up to something of importance, and she decided that the next round of telephone calls could wait while she answered the question he asked—

"Please, Janet, tell me—what else did my boy like?"

Dreadful Language

IT TOOK me a long time to learn the meaning of all the bad words I heard as a child. I was eight when the first one came my way. It happened one morning when my friend Evelyn and I were sitting at water's edge near my grandparents' summer house. My parents had gotten separated a few months earlier, and my mother was trying to make up for taking us away from Dad by letting us have Cokes at the beach, and in my case, inviting a friend to join us for the day.

"If that's what *you* want," I told her. "I don't care."

Evelyn arrived in spite of my indifference. Our hips and legs sank further beneath the sand with the ebb of each wave.

"Do you know what 'bitch' means?" she asked.

"A female dog," I said matter-of-factly. I knew it had another definition, but I wasn't going to let her bait me into saying it.

"You're a piece of work," she snickered. "How about 'shit'?"

I made a face. "I don't want to talk about this anymore."

There was a pause. The lifeguard blew his whistle at some teenagers who were swimming too close to the jetty.

"I overheard a man say 'fuck' yesterday," Evelyn said.

"Big deal," I said. I'd heard this one, and I believed it had to do with men and women and nakedness—but I wasn't entirely sure what it meant. She clearly did, though. She didn't seem like a child when she said it. She lowered her voice to accommodate the scope of this particular blasphemy, and her eyes glittered like ice under a streetlight. I was chagrined that she knew something I didn't, even if it was knowledge I could live without. "I hear people say 'fuck' all the time," I claimed.

"Ssh. Don't say it out loud."

"I will if I want to."

She cocked her head and looked at me shrewdly. "You don't know what it means, do you?"

"Of course I do."

"You're faking."

"So define it."

"You."

"You. Or else I'll scream it so everyone can hear," I said.

"You wouldn't."

I stood up. Clumps of wet sand slid down my thighs and hit the ground with a smack. "This is your last chance," I warned.

"No, Frannie . . ." Evelyn scrambled to her feet.

She'd reverted to being a child again and pleaded with me to be quiet, or else she would get my mother. It was time to make her pay for all her taunting.

"Fuck!" I shouted. Then I shouted it again, over and over. Even after Evelyn ran off I kept going, shouting at the sky, the ocean, the horizon, until my mother appeared and hauled me off the beach. On the drive back to the house she told me, with a discernible, pained tremor in her voice, how surprised she was by my behavior.

"I'm surprised by yours," I said. She knew what I was referring to.

There was a silence.

"Frannie, I have my reasons. Someday I'll explain it to you."

I stared out the window. There could be no good reason for leaving my dad.

"So what does 'fuck' mean?" I demanded.

I could tell she wanted to give me something, and sure enough, she gave me that. I didn't let her see I was sorry I'd asked.

Not long afterward, my father was killed in a car accident. I was standing right next to my mother when she got the news.

"God damn it," she said after she hung up. She slumped down the wall to the floor. "Shit, shit, shit!" she banged her thigh.

"What, what?" I was frightened. She never spoke like that.

She told me.

"Why are you so upset?" I demanded. "I'm the one who loves him!"

"Jesus Christ, Frannie." She covered her face with her hands, and I went up to my room. "No, no, no," I wrote on my blotter. I was ten, and buried. "Shit" didn't even begin to cover it.

After that, I thought I knew everything, but there was more.

A few years after my father's death, my mother remarried an older man named Denton Vaux, and I felt saved from the scattershot existence we'd been muddling through in our apartment—my mother had had to sell our house—near the railroad tracks in Wynnemoor. Denton was rich from inherited money and didn't have to work, yet he went to an office every day and sat on the boards of all the big civic institutions in the city. He wore ascots and good clothes even to putter around the property, and there were pictures of him with President Eisenhower and Elizabeth Taylor and other famous people and presidents tucked modestly between the pages of the heavy art books in the den. In my opinion he was a person of substance, and I looked forward to our lives settling into a proper routine again under his influence.

Instead, my mother became friends with Lena Schmidt.

I don't know how they met—I assume it was at a

party—but their friendship developed rapidly and intensely and soon it was difficult to remember what our house was like before Lena became a fixture in the living room. She had a husband, but he seldom came over with her, for which I didn't blame him one bit. On the rare occasions that he did show up, Lena managed to create the impression that he didn't need anyone's attention, and he ended up sitting in a deep, smothering chair and leafing through magazines until she was ready to leave. I pitied him, because I didn't trust her from the start, her and her heavy perfume, and the menacing switch of her skirt as she strode across the floor, and the way she hummed to herself. She was trouble—why couldn't anybody see it but me?

One day, soon after she appeared in our lives, I was sitting in the den (writing in my diary about how much I missed the boy with whom I'd fallen in love over spring vacation) when she barged through the front door without even knocking.

"Hello? Anyone here?" Her voice shone. I cringed.

"Come in," my mother called from the bedroom. "I'll be right down."

"Okay!"

Lena was from Brazil and had an accent both clipped and lilting. She made her way to the living room where she dallied over my mother's things, touching, examining, judging. I followed her progress, disapproving of every gesture. Her short, aggressively blunt-cut hair was clearly dyed a phony blue-black, and her clothes were blatantly suggestive. As if sensing an enemy, she cocked her head and looked around suspiciously until she spotted me. Then she affected a smile and walked over, proffering a handshake. Automatically I stood up, my diary clutched to my chest.

"Ciao, Frannie. I hope you are writing about a love affair."

"How did you know?" I was flushed and confused at having been found out. Even my own mother hadn't noticed I was in love.

"I can see it in you. You are a lover. I am, too. It takes one to know one."

She winked at me and touched my face. I suppose she was trying to establish some kind of rapport, but her familiarity made me cringe. A lover? I'd kissed my boyfriend, nothing else. I didn't understand what she meant by that, and I found it rude and intrusive. Thankfully my mother appeared. I ran upstairs with their laughter exploding behind me in vanquishing bursts.

Each afternoon after picking up her children from school, Lena came over and sat cross-legged on the living room floor with my mother, and the two of them talked and giggled like carefree girls. Not only giggled—they laughed, too, loudly, in great obliterating brays. That reckless laughter filled the house; I couldn't even read when she was over. It bothered me that the others didn't mind.

"She's not a good person," I told my mother.

"What makes you say that?" She was putting the plates on the dinner table while I lay the silver. The cook was on vacation.

"She's utterly selfish." I looked at my mother for a reaction, but she had on her poker face. I risked going on. "I don't think she really cares about you. She's just using you."

"For what?" She didn't seem too upset by my claim.

"I'm not exactly sure." My mother started toward the kitchen. I thought quickly; I wanted her to listen. "Well, for one thing, you live in a big house and she's in that shack. I don't think that's exactly her style." Lena's husband had lost his money in a bad land investment and they'd had to move to a town nearby where the scholarship kids in my class lived. "Don't think she doesn't like coming over here and hanging around. Not to mention getting to know Denton's friends."

Suddenly, shockingly, my mother began to cry. "Lena's my *friend*," she said in a hushed, hurt voice. "She *likes* me. I haven't had any fun for so long, and the moment I do, you begrudge it. Talk about selfish! You're really heartless, Frannie."

"You're making a fool of yourself," I pressed.

She looked away from me. "Maybe. But I need this."

"Don't say I didn't warn you," I said.

"I'd never say that." She lit a cigarette and blew a puff of smoke right past my cheek. "Let me clue you in, Frannie. We're all fools."

"Some of us more than others," I said.

She wiped her face with the heel of her hand. "It's hard for me to believe you're my child."

"At least we agree on something," I said.

No one, not even my mother, knew about Lena's affair at first. She continued to come over as usual and gradually, as spring became summer, the women's ongoing afternoon party moved out-of-doors. We had a tennis court, a swimming pool, and a large expanse of meadow and wood, so there was no shortage of places to play. After school let out for the summer, Lena began to bring her children over right after breakfast and left them with us all day. My mother went almost as nuts over those children as she had over Lena and often sat down for a game of checkers or Parcheesi with one or the other.

"See? You're their baby-sitter while she goes God knows where," I said hotly.

"What's wrong with you? Don't tell me you resent her *children?*"

"Not them—" How could I? They were as innocent as I was. "It's just that—" But I couldn't explain it. All I knew was that when I saw her and Lena's kids bent over a game board, my stomach turned to dough.

Lena sunbathed topless. She had long, tubular breasts that seemed anomalous springing out of her broad chest. When she first began to disrobe by the pool, my brothers made any excuse to wander out for a dip, but when the spectacle continued day after day they began to take it for granted to the point where they forgot about the peep show and were surprised when their friends ogled Lena.

I, on the other hand, never got used to it. I couldn't peaceably sit there with those breasts—especially not after they were joined by my mother's, which, although rounder and prettier than Lena's, were even more unsightly to my eyes. My mother bought a bikini. She wore the top at first, but one day I came home from a friend's house and saw that sorry strip of material lying face down on one of the wrought-iron tables by the pool, the beige foam cups stiff as a pair of candy dishes.

I tried not to look, but it was like trying not to rubberneck a car accident on a highway. Inevitably, my gaze was drawn to the gruesome scene. I wanted to tell her to get some sense in her head and cover herself up, but I knew she would tell me I was "uptight," a term she was using a lot at the time. Instead, I began to steer clear of the whole extravaganza. Whenever I heard her and Lena laughing, the ice clinking a hollow melody in their glasses of cold gin, I avoided the pool entirely, with the result that the only time I was free to swim in peace was early in the morning, when the surface was littered with dead bugs.

It was Lena's idea to have a tennis tournament at our house. She made a list for a round robin and had a local art student do it up as an official-looking chart on a piece of poster board. All the usual suspects signed up, and on every afternoon that it didn't rain, our property echoed with the twang of rubber on catgut; from my room, it sounded like a desultory war.

I got roped into signing up, because Denton asked me to, and I watched the preparations with my fingers crossed for his sake. My mother bought a table with an umbrella in the center of it and set it in the half moon of grass at the side of the court, so everyone could relax and get "tight" (Denton's term for drunk) while they waited for their turn to play. Denton loved all the activity and made no objection to shelling out for cases of liquor and buckets of iced shrimp and big bowls of fresh peaches and strawberries. Unbidden, he acted as emcee and umpire and patrolled the court in an ancient yellowed tennis sweater, with a Liberty print ascot at his throat. Behind his back, Lena made fun of him, but she flirted with him when he turned around. She flirted with everyone. Often the tableau at courtside looked like a scene from a forties movie where a comely USO girl is flanked by a gaggle of appreciative GIs.

Behind their backs, Lena talked about all the men as if they were silly.

"So why do you flirt with them!" I asked.

"You think I'm a hypocrite, don't you, Frannie?"

"You said it, not me."

"I'm not, really, although I don't deny I might be

something worse. I flirt for the same reason I play tennis. For the exercise." She laughed.

"What about women's lib?" I asked. She exasperated me. "Don't you believe in that?"

"I believe in having fun. I think that's as liberated as it gets, short of being a mystic."

Our tête-à-tête was cut short by the arrival of a new batch of competitors. I walked down to the stream where my sibs and Lena's girls were gathering garnet rocks and chopping out the stones with hammers and nails.

"If you think you're going to make a fortune from those worthless things, think again," I said.

They hung their heads as I dispelled their fantasies, but someone had to tell them the truth.

Because of Lena's policy of throwing everyone together in the round robin regardless of age or skill or sex, I had to play Freddie Sutton. He was a doctor who looked like a doctor—powerful and well scrubbed. We knew him through his wife, Bess, who was an old friend of my mother's, one of the school chums who was invited whenever we had a big party. Bess wasn't in the tournament; she was one of the few mothers who had a full-time job and therefore hadn't put in the hours on the club courts that were de rigueur for most of the women. Freddie, on the other hand, seemed to have time for everything.

I was nervous about playing him, especially as the match I was watching involved two men who each clearly wanted to cream the other; their aggressive vibes were not disguised by the way they tossed out perfunctory compliments on each other's successful shots. Though I was good enough at tennis, I didn't think I'd bear up very well if Freddie wanted to cream me.

I was sitting under the umbrella with my mother, Lena, and Denton when Freddie pulled up. He parked his car on the road beside the tennis court rather than leaving it in the driveway as everyone else did. He had a chocolate-brown Mercedes, the sight of which caused many rolled eyes among my mother's crowd, who only drove dowdy station wagons or Volkswagens, cars that they could pass on to their children or their cleaning women without having to live with the sickening thought of what they could have got on a trade-in. According to my mother, the Mercedes was evidence of an ego problem.

"Freddie must be having a midlife crisis if he needs a car like that," she diagnosed.

I hated it when she was judgmental, hated the way her searing opinions could color my views. I watched him with an eye to his state of mind as he locked his car and loped down the hill, his new sneakers squeaking on the lush grass. He sucked his gut in as he approached us.

"Who on earth does he think he's fooling?" my mother said. She made a knowing grimace at Lena, who giggled. But when Freddie came through the gate—

leaving it opened behind him, as if he were followed by the ghost of his surgical team, ever poised to do his scut work—Lena jumped to her feet and turned her beaming face his way.

Denton walked over and shut the gate.

"Lena," Freddie said. "I didn't know you were going to be here today."

"Oh, I was just about to leave, but my children are still in the pool."

Unsupervised, I might add, which constituted another black mark on her public record. When my mother once said something about it—like maybe it would be a good idea to keep an eye on them—Lena replied that she didn't believe in hovering. I laughed when I heard that one, but my mother thought it was enlightened. She began to go out without hiring sitters, and I had to pick up the slack.

"I'm glad you're here, Lena. My competition looks pretty fierce." He indicated me with a wave of his tennis racket. "I could use a cheering section."

"I'll cheer for whoever's winning," she said.

And cheer she did.

She sat at the table and drank Cuba Libres through our entire match. When we changed sides, I heard her ice rattling in Denton's mallard tumblers. At first she clapped for both of us, but by the end—when her kids were loitering at the net, whimpering with hunger—she was openly expressing her preference. I served the last game, and she squealed with excitement when I double-faulted. I had no one on my side. My mother and Denton had gone in to change for dinner, and everyone else had left hours earlier. I can't say for sure that Lena contributed to my loss, but her vivid, enthusiastic support for the away team didn't help. I got a tiny bit of revenge, though; when I lost, Freddie tried to jump the net to shake my hand, but the toe of his sneaker caught on the canvas tape and—poor thing—he fell onto the gravelly clay surface of the court.

Lena scrambled to help him up.

"Are you okay?" I asked. He was old, after all.

"I'm not sure." He grimaced and grabbed his leg. "Lena—I think you'd better drive me over to the emergency room."

"I'll get Mummy to follow you," I said.

"No!" They both barked.

"On second thought," Freddie said, "maybe you could just drive me up to the drugstore and I'll buy a few supplies to calm this knee down."

Lena smiled at him, a toothy smile that gave me the creeps. She turned to me. "Frannie, do you think you could watch the children until I get back?"

What choice did I have?

Off they went, Freddie leaning on Lena's shoulder. There was something about the way they were touching that seemed to surpass the medicinal purpose they'd claimed.

"Come on, kids," I said, instinctively protective. I led them back to the house, where Denton made them

54

Shirley Temples and we all sat in the living room and watched the daylight fade. Finally the cook called us to the table. Freddie and Lena reappeared as we were eating dessert. Her children jumped up to greet her and she embraced them and fawned over them as if they had been apart for months.

"Thank you for watching my little angels," Lena said.

"How's your knee, Dr. Sutton?" I asked. I didn't want to look at her.

"Much better, thank you. Or no thanks to you, I should say." He smiled at my mother. "Frannie gave me quite a runaround this afternoon."

My mother stared at the two of them, her mouth closed tight, her napkin pressed against her abdomen. I didn't know exactly what had happened, but I knew that I was finally being proved right about Lena. For once, I ate dessert.

Later that year, Freddie and Lena left their respective spouses. Wynnemoor was scandalized, and everyone sided with Freddie's wife, who blamed my mother for introducing the pair and abetting the lovers in their trysts.

"I didn't know," my mother said tearfully to anyone who would listen. "I didn't know, and by the time I did, there was nothing I could do about it."

She was frantic to be believed, but when people spoke against Lena, my mother defended her.

"She's from a different culture. She's not a Puritan

like we are. She's very passionate," I heard her say into the telephone.

"That's one way of putting it," I smirked, and she waved at me to shut up.

Lena and Freddie stayed together for about a year, and then Freddie came home. Everyone said Bess was a saint to forgive him.

"Forgive him? Don't kid yourself. She'll make his life hell," Denton predicted.

That sounded fair to me.

Lena and her children moved to New York where she quickly married Blaise Whitman, who was much richer than Freddie and Denton put together. We saw her infrequently after that. My mother, meanwhile, was still ostracized in certain circles for her part in the affair. She blamed Denton for not backing her up when she proclaimed her innocence, and he blamed her for being discontent in spite of all he'd done for us. No one cared at all what we children did after that, and the younger kids began to run wild and got bad reputations and warnings from the heads of our schools. I went in the other direction, retreated into my books, and advanced in every area, including tennis. By the next summer, I could have beaten Freddie easily; but we didn't have a tournament and I had to settle for playing my mother, whose game had gone so far off that, to create a little competition, I purposely hit ground strokes when I could have blasted her at the net.

Time didn't heal my mother's wound; she still missed

Lena. I saw her wince the night Denton settled himself at the dinner table and announced that he'd bumped into her and Blaise at the art museum.

"She hasn't called me," my mother said quietly. She had her two index fingers on the edge of the table and was running them back and forth.

"She doesn't need us anymore now that she's rich," I said.

"Rich, but still a cheap slut," Denton pronounced.

Her name never came up in Denton's house after that. What more was there to say?

After college I moved to New York, rented my own tiny studio apartment, and gradually began to feel a salubrious distance from my family and my past; it was a chance to reinvent myself and start over again. I was ready to change, or to be more accurate, I had changed, and I was ready to show it, to be popular, to try new things, to stop being so judgmental of people, including myself. I was ready to try my hand at love, too, an aspect of life I'd avoided all through college by burying myself in the library. Then I had the thought one day that my father wouldn't want me to be alone, and that realization gave me courage to open my mind and heart. All right, I told myself, it's time to see who's out there. I was excited, even if I was digging my nails into my palms.

I didn't need courage to look for work, I had to in order to feed myself—Denton didn't believe in allowances past the age of eighteen. With the help of a new Brooks Brothers suit, I managed to parlay my degree in art history into a job at a gallery. I had a number of duties, most of them of the menial, dues-paying variety, including logging in and organizing the slides submitted by artists who wanted us to represent them. Early on I devised a new system for cataloging this work, and my boss was pleased with me. He asked for my opinion of the submissions, and as I hadn't been expecting the question, I was more forthright than I might have been had I had time to stew over a critique. His request was offhand, and I matched his tone, mainly because I didn't think what I said mattered. I didn't delude myself that he'd make his decisions based on anything he heard from me. Yet he kept asking, and within a few weeks, he requested that I only show him the interesting work from then on, the less the better.

"What if I miss something really great?" I asked, suddenly nervous.

"You won't. You've got a good eye. And there isn't anything really great out there."

So I kept pouring his coffee, but I also made after-work appointments with artists to visit their studios; and I began keeping track of who was buying what at the other galleries in town.

One evening I took the subway down to Tribeca, then a frontier of raw lofts. It was June, but August hot, and I fantasized while scuffing along the subway platform and up the worn steps about removing my shoes and going barefoot. Sometimes I wished I were an artist and could create a new persona for myself; barefoot girl in the city, perhaps, wispy, wounded, mysterious. I looked about as opposite from that as possible as I rang the bell of a decrepit building on Hudson Street. I looked like a banker, on purpose; I thought the greater the contrast between me and the artists, the easier it made the authoritarian aspects of my job.

There was a side of myself muted by this image, however. Sometimes I felt like telling the artists that I knew what they meant when they described the strange states of being they entered into as they worked, the ecstasies that came after twenty or thirty straight hours of standing in front of a canvas. I understand, I wanted to say. I don't know how I did—I hadn't painted since elementary school—but their descriptions of their flights into parallel realms made my ribs vibrate.

I was thinking of this as I traveled up inside the building, in a freight elevator so old and filthy that I had to stand well away from the wall to avoid griming my clothes. I'd been stirred by what I'd seen on the slides of this particular artist, a man named Micah Tole, and I wondered if I'd have the nerve to describe the depth of my response, or if I'd settle for making the usual noises about power and energy and brush technique and let it go at that. The elevator door opened into a huge space, empty and light, typical of other places I'd been in, on the clean side of some.

"Hello?" I called out. "Is Mr. Tole here?"

"Over here," a voice answered and directed me to keep walking until I found the person it belonged to on the far side of the loft. When I came upon him, he was standing next to a refrigerator that stood free of any kitchen context and seemed a majestic monolith by its clever placement. Next to it, also perfectly sited, was a bright lime bicycle. And next to that—him. I took in that he was struggling to open a bottle of wine with a Swiss army knife corkscrew. I caught a glimpse, and then he was obscured by a splash of potent white light that came from somewhere within. When I looked again, I saw with love, and my real life began.

"Shit!" he yelped as he shattered the cork.

"It's a good thing you can paint," I said. "You'd be a lousy waiter." What had happened to me? I sounded snappy, like another, breezy kind of girl.

"Can I paint?"

"You can fish."

He smiled. "You're not going to stroke my ego?"

"I'm willing to, after I figure out the most effective way to do it. I will say right now that your paintings make me . . ."

I lost my glibness then. He took a step toward me.

"What?" he pressed. "What do they make you?"

I wanted to be honest with him. There were a couple of paintings leaning against the wall behind him. "May I look?"

He held out his arm, bowing slightly.

For some time I gazed at the canvases, moving between them casually, capriciously, taking them in without being too serious about it, as if they were scenery I lived with and could mostly take for granted. What happened was that I became light, ambitious, full of ideas and possibilities; he filled me with energy.

"They make me feel good—like a better person than I usually am."

He said nothing, but went across the room and came back with a stack of postcards. They were invitations to old shows, with reproductions of his paintings on the front. He handed the stack to me.

I raised my eyebrows, forming a question.

"So you can feel better while we're out to dinner tonight," he explained.

Tolstoy said that every happy family is alike; and although it seemed that what Micah and I had between us was utterly original, I think that we were like other happy couples in exactly the way Tolstoy meant. Our whole was greater than the sum of our parts, and we had a sense that luck or grace was at play in our coupling; that we'd been beckoned forward from the ranks and rewarded; that we were part of a grand plan.

I felt I deserved the reward for having been so restrained up until then, but Micah said he didn't deserve me at all, which I must admit I liked. We disagreed on some things, but not much. He became a star at the gallery while I handled the business end of his career for him; and on the weekends, he taught me to paint. More than anything I'd ever done I loved being in the loft with him on a Sunday afternoon and hearing nothing but the beating-of-wings sound of brush on canvas and the honking of irrelevant, ridiculous cars far away. He taught me with patience and was endlessly inventive in the way he demonstrated various techniques.

"You'll make a great father," I said.

He frowned. "I've never wanted kids."

That threw me. I'd always assumed I'd have children; I'd never questioned it.

"I do," I said.

He looked at me. "I might as well tell you this, too— I don't want to get married."

"To me?" I blurted.

"To anyone. I'm one of those who-needs-a-piece-of-paper, it-doesn't-guarantee-anything types. Can you live with that?"

"I don't know." I could barely speak. A desolation opened up inside me.

There was a pause.

"I might be able to live with a child," he said, "if you do the dirty work. But marriage? Can I postpone a discussion of that for a while?"

That sounded hopeful. "For a while," I said.

That was the only stumbling point between us. Otherwise, our lives meshed; I had no qualms about making love with him, because I knew I'd be with him for the rest of my life. Sometimes I thought our relationship should be more difficult, that there should be more challenges to surmount, but I was content to postpone our struggles until the future. I didn't criticize his smoking or drinking, and I loosened up myself. I was young, after all. I could stay out all night and still go to work looking fresh and feeling alert.

We bought furniture.

I even posed for him.

I planned to take him home for Christmas and was ready to be proud and shameless about his long hair and his black, black clothes. He asked me to move in with him, calling it a pre-engagement engagement, and I'd agreed to do it. I was ready, in every way, to say yes.

He was killed on a Sunday morning. He went out on his lime bicycle for a paper and some bagels and was hit by a cab driver who hadn't slept in two days. Death was instantaneous, they told me, but I only found that a mild comfort. I was glad for him that he didn't feel any pain, but I did. I did. For a while I went on with business as usual, trusting I'd heal eventually; but time had the opposite of its predicted effect, and I felt less and less connection with my life as the months went by. It was like the period just after my father's death, when part of me believed he was away on a business trip, and that my mother was lying. I remembered I'd refused to cry, because that would make it real. I cried for Micah, but for ages couldn't shake the odd sensation that he was still somewhere nearby. In a weak moment, I called my mother.

"It's as if he's about to walk in," I said.

"He isn't. Do you want to see a doctor?"

I didn't make the same mistake again.

I stayed in New York until the gallery mounted a posthumous show of Micah's work. Everything sold immediately, and the money went to his family, based on an old will. I got not so much as a drawing, including the sketches he'd done of me. Thanks to my expert cataloging, every scrap was accounted for, and none of it was officially mine. I had nothing of his, not an iota, except all the leftover hopes.

Eventually, listlessly, I moved back to Wynnemoor and took an administrative job in the alumnae relations department of my old school. It was a relief to be in a familiar place, around familiar faces. In Wynnemoor, no one seemed strange at all.

I married Jamie Roberts as much for Denton as for anyone. Denton was pals with Jamie's grandfather—hunting, fishing, lunching-at-the-club pals, an association that predisposed him toward the idea of having Jamie as a stepson-in-law—but he liked Jamie, too, and that carried weight with me.

"He's made of the same stuff as the old man," Denton proclaimed, an endorsement if ever there was one.

"So you think I'm safe with him?" I asked. I was sitting on the edge of Denton's bed, talking to him as he rested. He still went to the club wearing his ascots, but he rested when he was home.

"He's solid. He'll take care of you," Denton said.

I winced slightly at hearing that, but only slightly. For the most part, Jamie's solidity was a magnet, and once we'd begun to see each other, I was inexorably drawn to him. He was handsome, in the way that a lot of the Wynnemoor men were—tall, thin, and fine-featured, with beautiful forearms and hands that made my hands restless. He'd become even better looking as he got older, I thought; he'd grow gray and rangy, and women would turn to watch him walk into a room, just as they still watched Denton. If I wasn't in love with him—well, I'd been in love. I'd had my fair share, if not more. It was too much to expect I'd ever feel the way I had about Micah again, but I could be decent to Jamie and have a good life with him. We had so much in common and wanted the same things: children, peace. He was nice to me, kind and thoughtful in a way that inspired my own kindnesses in return.

I knew he'd propose, and sooner rather than later. Denton had often said that any man who stayed with a girl longer than a year without announcing his intentions was not a gentleman. Jamie was a gentleman, no doubt about that. In all the ways I could think of, Jamie was right for me.

My mother wasn't as enthusiastic about my engagement.

"You don't have to get married. You could just live together," she said. We'd just come from a caterer, where we'd priced salmon and canapés.

"I don't believe in that." Not anymore, I didn't.

Micah's death would have hurt less if I'd been his widow.

"You don't know what you're getting into."

"I know as much as I can. And Jamie is my friend. We'll figure it out."

"You could at least skip the wedding. I'll give you money instead, and you can buy furniture, or do some traveling."

"I want a wedding," I said. "I want everyone to celebrate with us." I thought of a wedding as a doorway into adult civilization, a literal passageway, like a Chinese moon gate. I didn't want to miss going through it. It angered me that she who'd been married twice wanted to deny me the experience.

"All right," she said, "all right. I think the salmon, then. Steak is too ugly in the middle of the day."

Salmon it was. Denton walked me down the aisle, slowly to be sure; but his arm was firm as we linked and I felt he was giving me away only to connect me more permanently to the broader circle of his world, which added a meaning to the ceremony for me that I hadn't imagined. We had a beautiful wedding, a perfect honeymoon in Tuscany. We planned to live in the city for a while when we came back—property values in Wynnemoor had increased out of our range—but our parents surprised us by making a down payment on a modest little house on a quiet street. I immediately set to work on it, and by the time our first child was born, we were well settled. The baby—a girl, Sophie—had a sunny room that I painted a blush white that turned rosy in the late afternoons and peach-colored when the sun rose.

Jamie loved his daughter, and by our fourth anniversary, we felt quite pleased with ourselves. Not a harsh word had ever passed between us.

Our second child was a boy, and again we felt quietly triumphant; it seemed quite a feat to have made one of each. We named him William and afterward had even more to talk about in bed at night. There was no end to our interest in repeating what the children had said and done during the day, no end to our discussions about the pros and cons of television or karate class or swimming lessons.

I say discussions, as if they were debates; but, in truth, Jamie left the final decisions on what was best for the children up to me. He was content to be with them, to play and enjoy—he was the father who always showed up for fathers' days at school, who came out from the city for school plays and games, who helped with the Spring Fair. His dedication to parenting afforded me free time, and I began to paint again. I went to art school and rented a studio in a part of Philadelphia that was being revived by artists and creative young couples. I decorated it carefully, with things I loved, and painted the walls to look like the sea. I put a cot right under the window and spent hours lying there looking out at the nearby rooftops.

What did I think of? Painting and abstractions, ideas and shapes, Micah. He came to me more and more often and was so himself, so surprising and other, that I had to reason with myself severely on my train rides back to Wynnemoor to remember that I was making him up. Or was I? Has anyone ever known for sure the provenance of either art or apparitions? I was rational, not easily carried away, a stalwart suburban mother—but in my studio I could forget.

A force from beyond me took hold of my brush and guided it across the canvas.

I communed with Micah.

The first time I stayed over at the studio Micah was with me for the entire night. Did I sleep? Hard to say. I know I lay on the cot for the requisite number of hours, only getting up to go to the bathroom and scribble a note or two. But I cannot claim for sure exactly where I stood on the continuum between waking and dreaming. I went back through my entire relationship with Micah, trying to recall every minute, every conversation. Then I brought him into the present and pictured what my life would be like now if he'd lived. Lying on my cot, I somehow heard what Micah would say to me about my painting, and it stimulated me to push myself harder, to work, work, work. I began a notebook in which I spoke to him and recorded our imagined dialogues. I kept up with my responsibilities, of course, but every chance I could, I was back to my studio, back to my notebook, back to the deepest part of my life.

It was nobody's fault. I knew I'd never leave Jamie—I couldn't hurt him like that, or the children. But I dreamed of it, privately, harmlessly, alone. Not even my best friends knew how often I thought of Micah. Everyone thought Jamie and I were the perfect couple. I suspect they believed I didn't have it in me to long for more.

After Denton died, my mother moved to Maine, and we went up there to visit her for Thanksgivings and Augusts, often overlapping with my sibs and their families. Every year we looked her over for signs of a boyfriend, but she gave a mock shudder whenever any of us spoke of it, saying she was content to be alone. I didn't believe that for a minute. She too thoroughly enjoyed our visits to make credible claims for being a loner. Yet she had her quiet room, the world of her books, while I pined for my studio, my notebook.

"You're so lucky," I told her.

"So are you," she replied.

She didn't understand; no one did. Occasionally I had the horrible thought that I hoped Jamie would die first, so I could have some time alone. I didn't really want that, of course, but the thought came nonetheless; I made up for it by working harder than ever on the marriage and our family life.

One summer afternoon we were all out sitting on the deck when we heard a blast of music nearby. It was an intrusion common to the city—even on the main drags of Wynnemoor—but not here, please Lord, and I shook

69

my head at the specter of people who didn't know how to behave on the island. Sophie was fourteen by then and was sitting next to me writing postcards while I sketched. Will was playing Monopoly with Jamie, and my mother was grooming the pots of pansies, breaking off the dead blooms with an efficient snap.

"Why don't they go to the Vineyard?" I said to no one in particular. Sophie gave a polite but uninterested shrug. In the next moment the music cut off abruptly, only to be replaced by the strident blare of a car horn, which I assumed had nothing to do with us. I was sketching the meadow in front of me and the ocean beyond and was engrossed enough that I didn't see anyone approaching. I was still staring at my drawing pad when I heard my mother's watering can thump onto the deck, and a squeal from her unexpected guest. That squeal, the braying laughter—even after all the years since I'd seen her, it didn't take much to realize it was Lena. I tolerated her two-cheeked kiss and was proud when my children did, too.

"Did you just arrive?" my mother asked.

Lena pulled off her hat and combed her fingers through her black, black hair. "Oh God, I don't think so, but it's hard to remember. I kidnapped the boat and have been visiting friends along the coast. Blaise isn't with me."

My mother frowned, and I supposed she was disappointed that it had taken a while for Lena to get around to dropping in on her. Same old, same old.

"Which one's your boat?" Will asked. He was taking sailing lessons.

Lena named it, and we all knew immediately which one she was talking about. It was a far cry from the sleek sailing yacht I knew Will was picturing. It was more of an Ari Onassis type of vessel, and certainly the biggest, gaudiest tub in the harbor that summer. Typical, I thought.

"Am I interrupting?" Lena asked.

"God no," my mother laughed. "I've been praying for someone to come by who'll have a drink with me. This is a very sober group!"

"All *right*," Lena said, with the same emphasis the kids used. She pulled a bottle from her big straw bag. A Montrachet. My mother laughed again.

"You should come by more often!"

"I think I might need to."

This time, Lena was clearly dropping a hint. She and my mother exchanged a knowing glance, tacitly agreeing to save the subject for later.

"Actually, I was about to take the kids for a swim," Jamie said. He'd sized up the situation and decided the women should be left alone. "Come on, Will," he said.

"God dammit to hell," Will said, hurling his pile of money into the middle of the Monopoly board.

"Will!" I shouted. His swearing was new, or new to me. I hated it.

"Where'd you hear that?" Jamie asked calmly.

"It was in a book," Will said.

"Do you know what it means?"

"Sort of." Will was stubborn, a bit of a know-it-all.

Jamie laid his hand on Will's shoulder. "Come on, let's go get into our suits and I'll explain it to you. Then you can decide if you want to keep saying it or not."

I almost spoke, but Jamie gave me a look that begged he be allowed to handle it. All right with me. I handled enough as it was. As long as Will was made to understand.

"I want to stay here," Sophie said.

"Go with your father," I ordered, in the dead-end tone that cut off all prospects for negotiation. I wish I could do the same, but I felt I had to talk to Lena for at least a few minutes. Jamie and the kids left, and the three of us drew our chairs together and filled our glasses with wine. Lena sat silhouetted against the harbor, her vivid presence making the picturesque view—boats racing around buoys, sea and sky—smack of kitsch. I had to give her credit for her style. Or maybe I was soft from the Montrachet, which was delicious, well worth the risk of having to succumb to an afternoon nap.

"So how are you?" my mother asked.

To my surprise, Lena immediately began to cry. She cried for a good five minutes without even trying to control herself; it was extraordinary to see. My mother patted her back and handed her one cocktail napkin after the next. I was useless, trying not to look but peeking, wondering whether it would be crass to keep drinking my wine or not. Lena's sobs worked on me, al-most like a baby's, and I was beginning to feel frantic and desperate by the time she calmed down. My mother coaxed the story out of her. Blaise was in love with a young sculptress, or at least he wanted to live with her for a while to see if it was the real thing. If it turned out to be, Lena was going to take him to the cleaner's.

"You should," my mother said. "Although it would be hard to hurt a man who has that much money."

"That's why I took the boat," Lena said. "He loves the boat. More than the sculptress, I think."

"Sculptress, schmulptress. From now on, I'm calling her the potter," my mother said, and she and Lena brayed.

"Just hang tough," my mother went on. "I waited Denton out. If I'd left when I wanted to, I'd be in one of those apartment buildings by the railroad. He wouldn't have given me anything. You have children together, so he'll have to pay you."

"I want the boat, the house, custody—everything. Damn him!"

"God damn him to hell!" my mother proclaimed.

"Fuck him and his cunting potter!" Lena was perking up. I wished I'd gone to the pool.

"Shit on them all," my mother said. "Or at least most of them." She nodded at me.

"Leave it to Frannie to have the one good marriage around," Lena said.

"That's what you think," I blurted.

They looked at each other.

"There's nothing wrong between you and Jamie, is there?" my mother asked nervously.

"No, no. It's nothing, really."

Lena looked at me shrewdly. "There's someone else, isn't there?"

"Not really . . ."

"What?" My mother plonked her feet onto the deck and sat up straight.

"No, no, it's nothing like that."

They were waiting. What the heck. *In vino veritas.*

"It's just that I still miss Micah," I said.

I thought my mother'd be relieved—at least there was no real threat—but she frowned harder.

"Ah. I always knew you were secretly a romantic, Frannie," Lena said and patted her jacket pocket. "Shit! I keep forgetting I quit." She looked at me. "So how does Jamie feel about it?"

"He doesn't know," I said.

"But he does," my mother said quietly. "They always know. Denton knew."

Lena nodded. "I knew Blaise was thinking about the potter before he did."

"Not Jamie," I said. I was so careful, so discreet. And what did my mother mean about Denton?

"Yes, Jamie," Lena said. "Believe me, he knows."

"Then why hasn't he ever said anything?" My stomach was roiling, a sloppy ship.

"He loves you," Lena said. "You're a lucky woman."

"She is," my mother agreed. "Jamie's as loyal as they come." She looked at me. "Do you really think Micah would have made as good a husband?"

I bristled. Was she rubbing it in that he'd been dragging his heels about marriage? I'd always believed that in time he'd have come around, but I didn't think it was worth arguing this point with my mother. She wasn't waiting for an answer, anyway; they changed the subject to other people we knew and the tragedies that had befallen them since the last time she and Lena had compared notes.

"I need some air," I said and got no protest. I walked to the causeway where the water sluiced over glimmering rocks.

I knew it was true what they'd said, and that there was no point trying to avoid it. Jamie sensed, even as I lay in his arms, that I was often elsewhere, just as Denton had sensed that he couldn't compete with my father. Was that what had made him bitter? Would Jamie become bitter, too?

One thing I understood: I had become my mother, the person I resented most. I wanted to blame her for this, but I couldn't find the anger. Instead, I wondered what my father had done to make her leave him when she'd loved him so much.

I didn't know.

I'd never bothered to ask.

"Help me, Micah," I whispered.

For the first time, there came no answer, and I ached so badly I felt I might faint from the pain. I'd never hear from him again—*I never had.* He was dead, and so was my father. I had my mother, and Jamie, but . . . oh, I was exhausted, and the thundering water made it hard to think. I tried to manage the noise by plugging my ears, but it roared past all my efforts to protect myself, and I heard over and over in that furious spray words I'd never really comprehended before.

Regret.

Shame.

Loneliness.

The worst words there are.

The Jungle Lodge

TOGETHER the sisters walked down to the dock where the jungle guides were packing the canoes for a day trip to a native village. At a glance, Abby knew it had been Carlos in the next room the night before. She'd heard grunts through the wall when she'd woken from a bad dream, but she hadn't been able to match the guttural sounds to the people she'd met at dinner. Now half the mystery was solved; the rest never would be.

The woman had been one of a group from Boston who'd left via sea plane right after breakfast. Some of them had stayed on either side of her and Liz's ramshackle room, but Abby hadn't learned who belonged where. She ran through the faces she'd met at dinner the night before but couldn't pinpoint anyone in particular. They'd all been tall and tennisy and, at a glance, interchangeable. How had Carlos hooked up with one of them? She'd seen no sign of a pairing off. Yet she'd heard them moaning intimately, as if they were real lovers.

Their keenings had been dreamy, too; separate from daily life. Would the woman always remember him?

Abby wondered. Or would the incident seem too em-
barrassing to contemplate once she got back home? Perhaps she'd feel nothing, as if it never happened. Abby
thought that would probably be the wisest way to handle something so intense. Or maybe that kind of encounter was routine for some people?

On this end, at least, it seemed there'd been no
hearts broken or shame felt. Carlos looked full-throttle
pleased with himself, like a boy reappearing at a party
after a grope in the bushes. He was tall and powerfully
built with thick braids of muscles on his upper arms
and thighs that strained his pants. She'd assumed there
was a rule against the guides doing anything more than
flirting with the hotel guests. Apparently, she'd been
wrong.

"Lucky girls," he said as they approached. "Another
day and the water will be too high to go to the villages.
The Indians will move back into the jungle for a few
months."

It was January and the Amazon was rising. Several
feet of the stilts supporting the lodge's buildings had
disappeared since the day before. The sisters were up
near the headwaters in Peru, their stepfather's idea of
an interesting travel destination. At least here, Abby
thought, the air smelled clean. Further downriver, she'd
found the fetid stench sickening.

"Carlos is cute," Liz said in a low voice. "But those
clothes . . ."

"Vêtements manqués," Abby whispered.

"Exactement," Liz agreed.

It was a term they'd invented on a past trip to signify that odd style they'd observed in various places around the world of cheap synthetic versions of American clothes that couldn't quite be called copies. Every seam, every angle was slightly off, as if the pieces had been designed by a creature from another planet who'd heard about pants and shirts but had never actually laid eyes on them. Carlos was clothed in typical examples of the style, made all the more noticeable and jarring because he was otherwise very handsome. He had the look of a Welshman: black beard, blacker hair, and dark blue eyes. He'd been quite funny the night before at dinner, naming every sound questioned by the hotel guests and putting the most horrifying possible interpretations on it. A wild boar had cornered one of the Indians! A crocodile had gotten hold of a boy! A goat was writhing in the jaws of a giant python!

Abby had played along, grimacing and gasping. The evening meal was served in a rustic dining hall, with only thin screens between them and the night and a fifteen-foot python skin on the wall. There was a row of wine and beer bottles set down the middle of the table and everyone was allowed to drink as much as he wanted. Abby and Liz had each downed quite a lot, knowing that Sawyer wouldn't stand in their way; he'd never taken an interest in what they ate or drank or did, leaving all those details up to their mother. The sisters were younger than anyone else—Abby a sophomore in college, Liz a senior at school—but they'd kept up with the chat and had found the evening terribly funny. Afterward in bed they'd discussed each person in great detail—except Carlos, Abby suddenly realized. They hadn't covered him. In fact, when she thought about it, she realized they'd tacitly avoided the subject, which meant one of two things: either it was an accidental omission, a fluke of the way the conversation went, or else it was too threatening to mention.

Abruptly Abby grabbed for Liz's arm.

"What is it?" Liz asked.

"I thought I felt something move under my feet."

Liz looked at her with sympathy. "This isn't a great vacation spot for someone with snake fear."

"I know. They always find me." It was true. There'd been three summers in a row at camp when she'd been the only one to see a snake.

"Carlos will protect you," Liz teased.

"Right!" Abby matched her sarcasm but felt relieved. Liz couldn't like him too much if she was making jokes at his expense. Yet Abby didn't feel secure, either. From experience, she knew that misinterpreting Liz's cavalier pose could be a mistake.

There'd been an incident a few years earlier when Liz accused Abby of flirting with a boy she liked, and when Abby tried to defend herself, Liz went on to expose all her secret resentments. The memory of that fight still caused Abby's heart to drum against her ribs. What had

hurt the most was that Liz believed, and said she always
had, that Abby lived in a dream world and was clueless
about what really went on with other people. The accusation had sickened Abby. She'd searched her conscience
and found no truth in it, no truth at all. Yet what could
she say to refute it? All she could do was to display extra
care, extra consideration, in hopes that Liz would someday revise her opinion. If there was even the slightest
possibility that Liz fancied Carlos, Abby wanted to
make it clear that she would give way. Carlos wasn't
worth the price of her sister. She was on the verge of saying something to indicate this when the rest of the
group made a noisy, touristy entrance.

"What an asshole," Liz said darkly.

Sawyer came sauntering down the hill in knee-high
rubber duck boots, a white Sulka shirt, khakis, and a
black bowler. A *velvet* bowler.

"White man in the tropics," Abby said.

"Ma knew what she was doing when she passed this
up."

Abby flinched at the bitterness of her tone. "Get off
his case, will you? He's not hurting anybody."

Liz made a face that said she disagreed but didn't
want to argue the point. As Sawyer approached she
walked a few feet away and struck up a conversation
with a woman from Texas named Bobbi who'd been the
liveliest of the live wires at the table the night before.
Sawyer was in the company of a young couple who were

drinking him in as if he were part of the atmosphere
and gazing at him with bald admiration—or condescension, depending on one's perspective.

Abby had seen this look on the faces of strangers before; what a wonderful old man, it said, isn't it amazing
how spry he is, and how with it. Her heart shrank as she
watched Sawyer's reactions. At first he looked pleased;
but gradually a pinch of annoyance settled around his
mouth and he tried to politely extricate himself from
the encounter. Abby knew what was happening. They'd
reminded him that he was notable now mainly "for his
age." Such adulation was liable to throw him into a
state of uncharacteristic despair. After one of these
episodes, he'd told Abby he didn't feel amazing to himself. He felt the way he always had. Even when he
looked in the mirror, he didn't mind what he saw. As far
as he was concerned it was the same face; narrow, finely
featured, handsome. It took others to remind him that
this familiar, pleasing mirror image was, objectively, the
face of an old man.

She caught his eye just as Carlos assigned him to a
canoe with the young couple. He raised his eyebrows in
an expressive circumflex that bespoke his consternation
at this turn of events. Abby gestured her willingness to
trade places, but he answered with a shake of his head,
releasing her from the bonds of obligation that made
her feel she should be entertaining him by providing
bright company on the trip as he was entertaining her
by paying for it. She gave him another nod imparting

her sympathy and climbed into a canoe with Liz and Bobbi. A guide named Hugo manned the stern with a hand-carved paddle.

"That old man was giving you the eye," Bobbi said to Abby.

"He's our stepfather," Abby said.

"You're kidding. How old is your mother?"

Abby decided to let Liz field this one, but Liz just gave out a high-pitched nervous giggle.

"Younger," Abby answered.

"She didn't come," Liz said. "She said she was no longer amused by Sawyer's using *National Geographic* as a travel brochure."

Because it showed what a "bloody-minded bastard" he is, Abby remembered her saying. She hated it when her mother was ugly like that.

"Never mind." Bobbi held up her hand, as if this information was being imposed on her against her will. "It's none of my business. Anybody want a doughnut? I missed breakfast."

"A doughnut? Where'd you get that?" Liz asked, as if it were a rare treasure.

"This is like camp," Abby said.

Bobbi opened her purse and began to spread a number of supplies on the floor in front of her. "I always travel with my own food. It's a good thing, too. Did you notice the color of the river? Not my cup of tea."

The sisters exchanged glances and laughed. They'd been raised to have a polite respect for local geographies and customs and felt liberated by Bobbi's irreverence. Soon they were all completely giddy. When Carlos popped by to make a final check on their canoe, it was all they could do not to laugh in his face. Again Abby was amused by the pastiche of Western clothing—a shirt dyed such a wrongheaded yellow that it looked as though it had been ruined by bad bleach, and a pair of ugly brown pants that ended in a rather half-hearted homage to bell-bottoms somewhere above his ankles. Predictably, his feet were clad in sandals, also of an ill-fitting sort that didn't seem to take the human body into account.

"Jesus meets Kmart," Bobbi said.

They let out a barrage of giggles that ricocheted around the clearing with the same piercing unexpectedness as the shrieks of nearby animals camouflaged within the vegetation. But the mirth drained from their faces as he aimed a powerful glance at each of them, one by one. What exactly constituted this power they didn't have time to ask themselves before they succumbed to it. When his eyes lighted on Abby for the second time he began to smile. Automatically she smiled back, but the feeling that passed between them as they gazed at each other confused her; perhaps he wasn't smiling at all; perhaps it was more of a smirk. She felt as though her shirt was buttoned wrong or her underclothes were showing.

Then her own blood began to roar past her ears, always a symptom of acute embarrassment. It was a trick she'd developed as a small child to drown out sounds that bothered her, but she'd learned to use it to submerge sticky emotions, too. It roared like a waterfall as Carlos stared at her. She glanced around at Bobbi and Liz in hopes of reestablishing the lightheartedness and camaraderie they'd shared a few moments earlier, but they looked equally stricken. There was a palpable sense of relief in the boat when Hugo dipped his paddle into the murky water and aimed them toward a jungle full of snakes, piranha, and crocs, all of which seemed comfortingly predictable compared to that unnerving blue-eyed stare.

Hugo was an altogether different sort: sweet, quiet, and not handsome at all. Abby thought it unfair that his looks—lack of looks—made him less compelling than Carlos, even though he was clearly a nicer man, but that was the way the world worked. Abby saw Liz and Bobbi fall in line with these conventions, relaxing in his presence to the point where they pulled their shirts and bra straps off their shoulders and exposed their bellies to get a tan. They traded sunscreen and lip gloss back and forth as he explained the sights along the riverbanks.

"Now you can't really make me believe you can tell one tree from the next," Bobbi teased him.

He laughed politely, and Abby shot him a sympathetic look. He gazed at her so gratefully that she turned around and faced him, gaining a new perspective that shrank the intimidating wall of the jungle to the status of a backdrop, which she found more manageable than having it loom before her as a frustrating, insoluble conundrum like a Zen koan. Relieved of paying attention to it, it occurred to her that she didn't really like the jungle. It was the opposite reaction of what she'd expected. She thought she would love it, in much the same way that she'd always loved the Caribbean, a landscape she felt she understood. Flora, thick, humid, overgrown. But it wasn't the same.

The jungle was too much, too monotonous. Even the birds were green—or most of them, anyway—and startled her when they flew from a branch and disturbed their camouflage. The trees were mind-numbingly tall and blocked out much of the sky. She found herself taking personally the way the vines strangled the tree trunks and identified with both predator and victim back and forth, first with the vines and their destructive forays, then with the trees and their witless resignation to the tedious, barely perceptible snuffing out of their vitality. It was an ugly place, really, ugly and cruel. And she didn't like the river either, for that matter.

Farther down, the Amazon had been the Amazon, wide and rather bland, but up where they were now near the headwaters, there was a mystery to it that she found unnerving. So much depended on it, so much life. She wanted it to be monumental, but in her mind's eye she found herself picturing the headwaters as a trickle of water that ran over one rock after another until it met up with another trickle, and so on; she saw it both abstractly and exactly, as a model something like that of the familiar twisted spine of the double helix. The trickles became streams became tributaries became the fat brown river, which itself became both a blessing and a threat. Soon the banks would overflow, and even as the local crops were irrigated, diseases would spread, people would drown, houses would be destroyed.

Abby hated the thought of being so bullied by nature; this was one place she would never want to return to again. A bug crawled onto her foot and she flicked it away. She was gliding through a world of true menace. If it weren't for the inane chatter of Liz and Bobbi, and Hugo's serenity in the face of their surroundings, Abby thought she would be very, very disturbed.

Hugo told his cargo that he was a doctor.

"Really?" Bobbi rose up from her sunning position and draped her freckled arms over the gunwales. "Where I come from the doctors are about the richest people around, next to the oilmen. You should move to Texas, hon."

Hugo looked confused.

"What kind of doctor are you?" Abby asked, trying to help him.

"I study infectious diseases among the jungle peoples," he said. "I work for the government eight months out of the year. Then I work as a guide to make money."

"Doesn't the government pay you?" Liz craned her head around to look at him.

"Not much. But it's important research," he said, shy but proud.

"All the more reason why you should be rich," Bobbi said. "You're letting the government take advantage of you. You seem way too bright a fellow for that."

Abby saw that Bobbi's shoulders were already getting pink. "Bobbi, you should cover up."

"Oh honey, I'm already too old to worry about ruining my skin. But thanks for thinking of me."

Abby exchanged glances with Hugo, who raised his eyebrows. She felt a rush of relief as she realized he'd got the whole picture.

"So what are you going to do, Hugo?" Bobbi asked.

"I have to take care of my people," he said simply.

"Well," Bobbi said. "In my book doctors and money go together. I meet a doctor who's not making money and I have to ask what's wrong with this picture."

Abby sprang to Hugo's defense. "Perhaps what's wrong with this picture is your point of view."

Instantly, she wished she could take it back, but Bobbi was nonplussed.

"You're right. What do I know outside of Houston?"

"No, I'm sorry. I went overboard." Abby placed her hands palm to palm and pretended to dive into the water. Bobbi and Liz laughed; all was forgiven.

"Thanks for reminding me to behave myself," Bobbi said.

"All's well . . ." Abby said.

". . . that ends well." Hugo finished the aphorism for

her. He flashed her a smile that displayed both his pleasure at knowing the saying and his gratitude to her for rescuing him. Abby saw both those feelings in his shiny brown face, but as they continued to smile at each other, she saw there was yet another response underlying all of what shone on the surface. She turned forward again and stared at the shimmering green wall. The jungle was so ridiculously thick that it seemed almost flat, like the painted frieze in Sawyer's dining room, a panoply of brush strokes that had often made her vision blur as the evening wore on. She had the kaleidoscopic sensation of the scenery falling over and over itself, forming patterns that made brief, provocative impressions before they disappeared. She hoped she'd been wrong about Hugo. Maybe it was the glare off the water that had made his eyes seem so piercing and bright.

She felt a wave of dismay that she might end up paying a price for her instinctive sympathy. She didn't want to have to deal with his feelings and possibly hurt them. *Leave me alone*, she thought, and concentrated on sending the message telepathically, a technique she'd used as long as she could remember, at school and other places where people crossed her boundaries. She knew it rarely worked, but she believed that was her own fault for not imbuing the phrase with enough power. Four times now, she gave it her all. When she turned around, however, he immediately tried to catch her eye again. She cast around for help; but Liz was sunning herself with her eyes closed and Bobbi was examining the freckles on her calf. Only Hugo was aware of her, staring as he dipped his paddle rhythmically.

"Tell me a joke," Abby said to Liz.

"All right. How about a knock-knock joke. You start."

"Knock knock," Abby said.

"Who's there?" Liz asked.

"How am I supposed to know?" Abby heard herself sound slightly hysterical.

"It's a trick. Don't you get it?" Liz was annoyed. She always got inordinately angry when Abby was dense.

"I remember that one," Bobbi said. "But I'm still partial to Sam-and-Janet evening."

Finally Abby understood. She felt slow and far away, but willed herself to join in. "That's a good one. I'll have to remember that."

Liz clasped her hands behind her head, exposing her chalky armpits to the sun. "I can't believe you haven't heard it before."

Abby shrugged. "Well, I haven't." There was an awkward pause. What was happening? She didn't want to squabble. "But have you heard the one about the three-legged pig?"

For the rest of the ride she joked with the other women while studiously avoiding Hugo's eyes. But that didn't prevent him from watching her—she felt his gaze, steady and constant. Somehow, without meaning to, she'd given him hope.

. . .

The native village left little to the imagination. The huts were completely open air with no walls or reasonable facsimiles thereof anywhere in sight. Basically they consisted of four posts topped off by a roof made of wood poles and leaves and a platform a few feet off the ground that supported the people and all their belongings.

The guides led the group from hut to hut explaining local customs as they went. Abby was appalled by the whole spectacle. She'd always been the kind of girl who empathized with the animals in the zoo while sustaining an obdurate incomprehension of their keeper's motives. As far as she was concerned she had no business watching these women nurse their babies and cook their lunch; she got no thrill from seeing the men swinging lazily in their hammocks, smoking whatever they were smoking and sucking on nuts that stained their lips red. Hugo was respectful and delicate in his description of their lives, but still Abby thought it voyeuristic. The only thing that made it bearable was Liz's similar take on the excursion, which she made known by means of a steady stream of ironic comments about conquistadors and manifest destiny.

Bobbi poked around at will, effectively creating her own tour, occasionally popping back into the group to say she'd just spotted a pair of pink nylon panties hung up to dry on the far side of a roof or that she'd noticed an odd echo as she walked across a remote stretch of the compound, which she construed as being evidence of an underground bunker that no doubt housed the TVs and washing machines.

"Any questions?" Hugo asked.

"One big one," Bobbi said. "I'm sure we're all wondering the same thing, so I'm just going to say it aloud. Where on God's earth do these people go for a little privacy?"

Hugo waved his arm to indicate the vast secret hiding place that was the jungle. Everyone automatically looked, even though there was nothing to see.

"No, thank you," Bobbi said. "I wouldn't lie on my back in that mud puddle for all the money in the world."

"How about for Brad Pitt?" Liz asked.

"No way. Maybe John Travolta. Although he seems a little goofy."

Abby edged away from the banter and found Sawyer. Together they walked down to the river to watch a listless demonstration of how to carve a dugout canoe.

"I've seen this so many times in so many places," Sawyer said. "I could make a canoe with my eyes closed."

"When I was in third grade I made a cave tool that was the best one in the class," Abby said.

"It seems we're well equipped to survive here if we get stranded."

Abby thought of Hugo's arms, the lean muscles moving under his skin as he pulled on the paddle. "I think it might take a bit more than those particular skills."

Someone whistled and a swarm of male children

gathered at the top of the muddy hill. They tore down the slope and dove naked into the awful water, their backs and butts slick as dolphins. Everyone clapped. Somehow the tourists were made to understand that they should throw coins; the boys dove for them.

"Ugh," Abby said.

"Veni, vidi, vici," Sawyer joked. He put his camera to his eye and took a picture of a boy hanging in midair like a boomerang over the water. "Where's your sister?"

Abby said that the last she knew Liz was strolling around with Bobbi. She scanned the clearing. "There they are." They were talking to Carlos. He said something and they both laughed.

"Is she enjoying herself?" Sawyer asked.

Abby would have said yes in any case to make the old man feel his money had been well spent, but it was clearly true, at least at the moment. There was not a trace of gloom or worry in Liz's face as she stood across the glen with Bobbi and Carlos. She looked utterly at home in this bizarre outpost; the jungle suited her.

"Yes, she's having a great time."

"And you?" he asked.

Although she was too far away to hear, at that moment Liz turned toward them and cocked her head, as if curious how Abby would answer.

"Everything's fine," she said. Liz looked quite splendid, she thought, splendid and . . . separate.

"You two seem to be getting along," Sawyer continued.

93

"Uh huh." She and Liz had been so close over the past week that she'd come to assume a degree of likeness between them that gave short shrift to all their secrets. Yet suddenly a secret had arisen, pushing them apart.

"Long talks and all that?"

"It's been like one long slumber party," Abby said. She sensed he was hinting at something, but she was too distracted to intuit what it was. As she continued watching Carlos and Liz, she felt the sickening humiliation of being the last one left standing in a game of musical chairs. Liz pushed up on her tiptoes and whispered something into Carlos's ear. Hands on hips—very strutting, very manly—he nodded. Then he looked over at Abby and smiled. Or was it a smirk? She gave a wobbly smile back, then cut her eyes away when his stare made her uneasy.

"She's quite a flirt isn't she?" Sawyer clucked his tongue.

Abby had no chance to answer before Carlos approached. "The men will invite you to take a turn with the blowgun," he said to Sawyer. "She thought you would want to try."

Liz raised her hand in a fist. "I dare you," she called out.

"No, Sawyer, it's too heavy," Abby said. They'd all been encouraged to lift the blowguns as they toured what served as a munitions hut. The weapons were at least nine feet long and weighed upward of sixty awkward pounds.

"I'm not so sure about that." He looked across the glen.

"Come on Sawyer, you're the man!" Liz challenged.

"She's just teasing," Abby said, annoyed with Liz for putting this stupid game in motion.

"The men will honor you if you do it," Carlos said.

Abby gave a small disapproving shake of her head, for which she was rewarded with another of Carlos's smirks. This one made her blush.

"I'm game. You only live once," Sawyer said.

"Good!" Carlos rubbed his hands.

They all walked to the clearing where the native men were making their preparations and laughing as they filled their cheeks with darts. Hugo materialized at her side and assured her that these particular darts weren't poison tipped.

"Thank God for small favors," Abby said wryly.

He was perplexed. She considered explaining but she knew from experience that she was a washout at unraveling idioms—and she didn't want to segue into a conversation about religion. "Never mind," she said. "Thank you for telling me."

She gave a neutral smile. He lay his hand on her shoulder, where it pressed on her heavily. The men blew their darts, their breath sounding a thump in the hollow barrels just as the missiles arced across the clearing into the target tree. Then it was time for the tourists to have a crack at it. Sawyer stepped right up.

"Please be careful," Abby said.

He got one end of the pole to his lips but the tip remained stubbornly south of his waist. "Try again. Start from the beginning," Carlos instructed.

"He's a fine man." Hugo gave Abby's arm a consoling squeeze.

"Yes," she said briskly and held herself stiff.

Sawyer hoisted the pole again. This time he got it nearly straight.

"Blow now!" Hugo called out.

The dart shot from the tip and landed in the mud a few feet from the tree line. Hugo rushed to take the pole from Sawyer's hands, thereby relieving him of a possible anticlimax to his victory. Everyone clapped. Bobbi ran forward and hugged him and the couple who'd admired him earlier behaved as though it was their victory, too. Only Liz seemed unmoved by this brave showing. In the midst of all the fun Abby spotted her standing alone, her arms tightly crossed.

The trip to the village, if nothing else, had served the purpose of bringing the group together, so that when they went in to dinner that night, there was much laughter and teasing back and forth even before they made a dent in the array of sweating bottles. Carlos was particularly convivial. His clothes were as unfortunate as ever but his manner was suave. Officially he was seated between Sawyer and Bobbi, but every time he returned from the buffet table he plunked himself down beside someone else and gave them his exclusive, if brief, attention. What an operator, Abby thought.

She watched him turn the charm on and off with the mechanical regularity of a traffic light and was embarrassed to recall how his cheesy stare had rattled her earlier in the day. There was really nothing to it, unless pomposity and egotism could be construed to have dimension. He was a jerk, plain and simple. At home she wouldn't have looked at him twice. It was the jungle, the disorienting jungle, that had tricked her into making more of him.

She consoled herself that she wasn't the first to have made a fool of herself in unfamiliar terrain. Nothing had happened, either—at least nothing tangible. She doubted she'd think of him again once they went away.

Poor Liz, though. Clearly she'd had no such revelation about him. When he went to sit by her, she lit up. He didn't know, of course, that she was rarely as animated or full of lighthearted laughter, and it irked Abby that he was the one to have brought her out. But what harm could it do for her to believe he sincerely shared her interest? He certainly couldn't visit her bed that night, not with Abby two feet away. An evening of burning glances, a dance or two and maybe a kiss, then back to Lima in the morning. There was no reason for her to ever know he was a cad.

So be it, Abby thought. Willfully she shook off her vigilance and allowed herself to simply absorb the scene, drink the beer, and speak aloud to the nearby company whatever absurdities came into her head. She'd just told Liz's knock-knock joke when Sawyer came and sat down next to her.

"Who do they think they're fooling?" she said. She leaned woozily on his shoulder. "I bet that isn't even a real snake on the wall."

Sawyer nodded. "With this kind of place, the second it stops being exotic it's completely tawdry."

"Exactly!" Abby said, surprised at being so completely understood.

"So you've seen through it. I'm not surprised. I think the scales have not yet slipped, however, from our Liz's eyes," Sawyer said.

Abby smiled. "You made a rhyme."

"I did, didn't I?"

"Anyway, I'd rather she didn't know," Abby said, then let out a screech at the sudden sharp chill on her back.

"Rather she didn't know what?" Bobbi asked. She proffered the freezing beer bottle she'd just pressed against Abby's thin blouse. Abby, though disgruntled, accepted it.

"Never mind," Bobbi said. "It's none of my beeswax. Dance?" she proposed to Sawyer and held out her hands.

He rose gallantly and maneuvered her body into dance position with the grace of a much younger man. They twirled off, laughing. Abby liked seeing him laugh. He didn't much at home.

He really is incredible, she thought.

Liz came by and touched Abby's shoulder. "I have to go to the bathroom. I'll be right back." She bent lower. "He's cute, isn't he?"

Together they watched Carlos pose near the center of the table, then dramatically sweep a bottle up and around in an arc before pouring himself another glass of wine.

Liz sighed. "I wish I could take him home with me."

"Mum would love that," Abby said.

"Then again, what does Mum know about men?" Liz asked.

It was a rhetorical question. Liz trotted off. Abby was alone then, contentedly so, and tapped her feet to the music as the others took to the floor. She smiled again at how Sawyer had called the lodge "tawdry." She realized she'd thought so from the start, but had tried to see beyond it because of all Sawyer had paid and how far they'd come. She reflected on the whole trip, her thoughts gradually taking up the case of travel in general; in her present mood, she could see only how silly it was. Ou est la double-vay say? Rickshaws. Lederhosen. She began to laugh, then saw Hugo watching her and stopped. He came over anyway. As he drew close, she saw he was drunk.

"Let's dance." He grabbed her wrist.

"No thank you. My feet are bothering me."

"Take off your shoes."

"I don't want to dance."

"Sure you do." He tugged at her.

"Not right now, Hugo. Maybe later."

"Please." He pulled at her again and she snatched her arm back with such force that it hit the table, hard. Hugo reached for her other hand. "I'm sorry, Abby. You are so beautiful."

She eased her arm into her lap. It was sore, but she'd broken no bones. "Hugo, please. I'm very tired."

"All right, Abby, let's only talk . . ."

Then Carlos was there, suddenly, his body between them. "Abby. I was going to show you the crocodiles. This is a good time." He put his hand under her elbow and helped her up.

"I'd like that," Abby said.

Hugo let go reluctantly. "Maybe later," he said, echoing her brush-off phrase.

Abby stepped backward. "I don't think so. Good night."

Carlos led her to a door at the far end of the room. He picked up a flashlight on the way out. "They come up after dark. I'll shine the light in their eyes so you can see them."

"You're serious about this?" She'd thought it a simple rescue.

He fixed his look on her. "It's part of the tour. You can't see crocodiles in Pennsylvania."

"That's a matter of opinion," she cracked.

"What?"

"Never mind. Why don't we wait for Liz? I know she'll want to see them, too."

"I'll show her later."

He walked in front of her onto the deck. There was a moon big enough to illuminate a desert landscape but in the jungle it was wan and negligible. "Now look out across the lagoon," Carlos said. "When I turn on the flashlight, you'll see their eyes shining."

He flicked the switch. A dozen orbs gleamed in the humid dark. It was an odd tableau, more than anything like an illustration in a children's picture book. In her mind's eye, Abby supplied the rest of the monsters, great masses of teeth and ridges of coarse hide protruding above the water. Yet she felt quite calm, neither afraid nor thrilled; the tawdriness had spread. Carlos played his role with gusto and behaved as if they were in some danger. "Get back," he hissed when she strolled to the rail.

Abby chuckled.

"Ah," Carlos said knowingly, "you're one of those who laughs in the face of fear."

He fingered her hair. She moved her head.

"I'm not afraid," she said. "But I am tired. Let's go back in."

He stared and breathed deeply. "Hugo is right. You are very beautiful," he said. And kissed her.

Immediately, Abby thought of Liz. "Stop it, Carlos. I'm not interested."

He kissed her again and turned fierce. She struggled to get away but his arms flexed with determination. "No, Carlos, no," she whimpered.

He pushed her onto the hammock and lay heavily on top of her. Then he tore at her clothes. He had his hand over her mouth and nose, so she could barely breathe. She stared at him, telegraphing a shriek of protest, but it had no effect. Then she just wanted it to be over with and settled into a detached lassitude that seemed almost comforting.

"Lie still," Carlos grunted, close to her ear. Then he did something that made her faint.

She could not wash it away, could not get rid of it. Her Swiss dot pajamas seemed wrong, clothes for a cleaner girl. How could she face him in the morning? He'd left her out there, by herself; when she'd come to, she'd been alone. She'd had to walk back through the dining room, reeling with pain, and overhear him flirting. She'd had to sense Liz staring at her suspiciously. She wished she could have warned her, but she'd been too shocked and embarrassed to do anything but hurry to the room. He wouldn't hurt Liz, though, Abby told herself, not if Liz was a willing partner. Or would he, anyway?

Everything ached, and she kept bleeding, using up all the washcloths and towels. In the mirror she watched herself dry her eyes and comb her hair with her fingers. The floor was gritty and splintery under her bare feet and she automatically curled her toes as she walked to her bed. It had begun to rain. The roof smelled spicy. Liz was still out.

Abby remembered reading that that kind of sex was

practiced by certain cultures as a form of birth control. Then she tried not to think, but her stunned body had a mind of its own. The moment when he entered her repeated itself over and over in her nerves so that her flesh would not relax but remained tense and strained with the memory of agony.

Finally Liz and Sawyer came clomping up the planked walkway. The spring on the screen door twanged as they entered. They were wet; it was raining again. Abby didn't want to talk to anyone, not now. She lay on her side and breathed steadily, feigning sleep.

"All right, Sawyer," Liz said testily. "I'm safe. Now go to your room."

"How about a kiss goodnight?"

Abby cringed. That tone . . .

"Go to bed," Liz hissed. "You're drunk."

"Don't be mean, Lizzo. You used to be such a sweet girl."

"Forget it, Sawyer. Go find someone else. Go away."

"Liz . . ."

Leave her alone, Abby prayed. She prayed, too, for Liz to understand he was just being silly and not hate him even more.

"I'll scream. I mean it," Liz said.

"One kiss."

"Go to hell!"

Abby heard a scuffle, then the sound of his footsteps receding across the bridge to his room in an adjacent building. She heard shoes clattering across the floorboards, a zipper, then the swish of sheets as Liz got in bed.

"Liz?" Abby whispered.

"I thought you were asleep."

"No. I was waiting up for you. I need to talk to you."

"If it's about Carlos, don't bother," Liz said. "He's a bug, just another bug that should be squashed."

"I didn't flirt with him."

"Fine. I don't care. Let's go to sleep."

Abby hesitated. It seemed dangerous to press the subject any further at the moment. She could reveal the rest in Lima—if she even wanted to. The thought of anyone knowing, even Liz, filled her with shame. She made a willful decision to change the subject.

"Sawyer was weird just now," she ventured. She thought if they talked about it, she could smooth things over.

"Abby, Abby, Abby," Liz said woefully. "You're so clueless."

"About what!" Abby said hotly. The accusation stung. "You can't just say that. Tell me what you mean."

Liz sat up. "What I mean, Abby, is Sawyer's always like that. Always. Now do you understand?"

It took her a moment, but then her guts writhed. "Oh, Liz," she said when she could speak. "I'm so sorry."

"I don't want to talk about it anymore. I'm going to sleep."

She lay back down and punched a spot for her head in the pillow.

"When did it start?" Abby asked.

"We were children," Liz said. "Now stop talking."

"Does Mum know?"

"I've never told her. Maybe. Goodnight."

Abby rolled into her sleeping position, but she was alive with nerves. Sawyer had sounded so slimy when he'd suggested a kiss. How far had it gone? Had he acted like this all during the trip? Why Liz and not her? How had he chosen?

The rain battered the roof hard, and Abby sensed the river climbing. Soon, she thought with dread, it would flood the banks.

Triage

IN HER sixties, Ella began to take courses in theology. She'd always practiced some form of religion or another—Buddhism had taken up the greater part of her spiritual life, after she escaped from the dour pews of Wynnemoor Presbyterian—but she'd never gotten a proper overview of the entire subject. Now restive, ambitious, and with time on her hands, she hit the books wholeheartedly and found she had a knack for it. She was the oldest student at the seminary but was thin and erect as a girl, and the bloom of new ideas filled her with vitality.

"No one has understood this before!" she would say excitedly into the telephone. On the other end of the line, dotted here and there across the country, her six children stood in their kitchens and living rooms performing whatever chores they could within their reach as they listened and periodically interjected their encouragement. Whenever they spoke to each other they remarked on how well their mother sounded lately, the best they could remember since their father died. She seemed almost sanguine. They'd grown up humoring her intermittent passions, and rather than resenting any pursuit that deflected her attention from them, they were always relieved when something interested her enough that her pervasive sense of disappointment ebbed.

Only Margie, the second daughter, was ambivalent about this latest development. When she heard her mother's voice, fevered and insistent, her stomach began to purl with the same combination of dread and titillation that she'd felt during Ella's later pregnancies, when she knew that what would be gained in the form of a miraculous addition to the family wouldn't sufficiently atone for the further division of Ella's time. But it seemed she was the only one of her siblings for whom these betrayals and abandonments remained an open wound. Everyone else had either gotten enough of their mother or gotten over it. Perversely, Ella sought the most approval for her new insights from Margie, who was the least able to mindlessly jolly her along.

"Why hasn't anyone thought of this before?" Ella asked after giving her latest brainstorm. It was a rhetorical question, the only possible answer being that no one was as smart.

Margie handed a toy to her baby daughter while coaching herself to be patient. "I think you've got something," she might say, or "that's an interesting way to think about it."

What harm could it do for her mother to believe she understood God better than anyone else did? The wisest course was to allow Ella to talk herself out about Him—she was like a teen with a painful crush—and then move on to more pertinent topics. Yet in spite of Margie's best efforts, the conversation always returned to the subject of religion, and all the secret anger of their relationship came to the surface.

"I'm tired of men," Ella began one day. "If only women would keep their legs together, we could fight back."

"I think women would do better to give up religion. It's the Judeo-Christian ethic that gives moral authority to the idea of a patriarchy."

Of course, when Margie said women should give up religion, she meant Ella, and when Ella said women should keep their legs together, she meant Margie. They'd always envied each other both their soulfulness and their sexuality and the envy had kept them from being either direct or supportive.

"It depends on your interpretation," Ella said. "Some people think Jesus was a feminist, and that his mother and Mary Magdalene were disciples on a par with the other twelve."

Margie's shoulders tightened. "I'm the one who said that to you."

"I don't think so."

"Where did you hear it?"

Silence.

"We had a long talk about this," Margie said. "I told you that was one of my theories. Jesus had an inkling of the possibilities of equality, and then Saint Paul came along and reinstated the traditional misogyny. Jesus was an anomaly."

"I think I heard it at the seminary," Ella said. "I'm sure some of the other women were talking about it."

Anger swept through Margie's body, but when she saw the baby watching her she quickly turned away, instinctively protecting Caroline from the rage she could feel twisting her features.

"Don't you remember?" she pressed. She named the time and the place of the conversation. As a child, she'd developed a memory for such things in order to stave off obliteration by Ella's tendency to assimilate the provenance of any idea or style that appealed to her.

There was a pause. "Well, it doesn't matter whose idea it was. The point is that it's a good idea." Ella thereby dismissed the wrangling over the theory's derivation, as if it were beneath her.

It did matter, though. It mattered to Margie that she'd had the idea, that she'd told it to her mother, and that her mother had found it good. But if Margie continued to insist the idea was hers Ella would call her egocentric and vain. Ella had many such tricks; Margie had internalized them so thoroughly that even when Ella was far away, she might as well have been in the same room, in the same bed, in the same head. Margie wasn't blind to the dynamic of the situation. She was well aware that her constant echoing of that belittling voice made it all the more powerful, but her analysis changed nothing.

This rash of theological conversations prompted Margie to think about religion again. She'd given it up years earlier when it seemed to effect a separation from the other parts of her life rather than affording the connection for which she longed. Now it all came back. Soon she was nearly as obsessed as Ella, and whenever her husband came near, she harangued him with her ideas. These were not conversations. They were monologues, diatribes, filibusters, because he already agreed with her on this subject and most others. She promised herself continually that she would stop bothering him with this stuff and cut straight to the complaints about her mother, which were more dangerous to keep to herself. She was afraid that if she didn't air the litany of grievances she had against Ella that they would gather and multiply and she would end up with cancer.

"I can't believe how much you've changed," Margie needled Ella. "I always used to tell you that Catholic theology was compelling, and you dismissed it."

"I don't remember that," Ella said.

"Surprise, surprise." Margie's voice was acid. She was tired from the baby, tired from her work, tired from living a life that was turning out to be as disappointing as her mother's, tired of trying to please her mother by leading a disappointing life, tired of justifying why she wasn't doing better. She used to read every night before she went to sleep, but now she turned out the lights the moment she got into bed and welcomed the languid slide into unconsciousness.

After one particularly bruising conversation Margie found herself praying for relief. Please God, she thought, please let me get away from her. No—that wasn't what she meant. Please God, she amended her supplication, let my mother see me.

She stopped abruptly. What was she doing? She didn't pray anymore. She didn't even believe in God anymore. She believed in nature. She believed that all answers to everything could be found in nature. She would tell Ella that and forever after drop the subject.

"Here's the way I think about the Trinity," she said the next time Ella called. "I think of it as an extended metaphor for a sperm and an egg coming together to make a baby. The man, the woman, and the new life they create are all utterly connected in that one moment. They are three, but they are not separate. Each person alive embodies this moment and is the ongoing unity of himself and his parents. Nothing religion says really improves on this. I think it's miraculous enough simply to see the thing for what it is."

Unexpectedly, Margie found herself crying. Caroline was at her feet, reaching to be picked up. Margie knelt by her as she held the telephone tight, waiting.

"What a lovely way of looking at it," Ella said.

"You like that?" Margie steadied her voice.

There was a pause. "I think it's terrific. I wish you

would do something with your ideas. You're wasting your mind. You don't have forever, you know. You have to think about yourself. Caroline will grow up, no matter how it seems now."

Margie stood and pressed fingers into her eyes, making bursts of light fly across her field of vision. When she opened them again, she saw that Caroline was crawling for the first time. The sight of her child's brute determination was heart-stopping.

"Just a sec, Mother," she said and tiptoed protectively alongside the lumbering baby. She was so moved and amazed and caught up in the moment that it wasn't until some time later that she remembered she'd left Ella waiting on the other end of the line. Margie retrieved the receiver, her chest aching with excitement. "Ma, guess what? Caroline crawled!"

"Now you're really in for it," Ella said. "Now you'll have to watch her every second. Be sure to block off all the plugs." She paused for the same amount of time it used to take her to pull in a lungful of smoke. She'd quit twenty years earlier, but her conversations still had a smoker's rhythm to them. "Let's get back to your idea about the Trinity. What about multiple births, especially fraternal twins . . ."

Caroline maneuvered onto her hands and knees and made for the doorway. Margie instinctively began to wave her back but thought better of it. Instead, she lay the receiver down again and unobtrusively followed her daughter into the dining room, a distance from which

Ella's precise words were indistinguishable, nothing more than a murmur, a swarm of bees pestering a growth of peonies, droning on and on, ad infinitum. Margie pulled the door closed behind her and the buzzing in her ears that had threatened to drive her to violence countless times in her life . . . stopped. Then peace came, but briefly. Ella was not giving up without a fight and the image of her that Margie carried in her conscience weighed in with the grim reminder that someday she would be dead and Margie would miss her very much.

"Fuck!" Margie said and banged her fist on the sideboard. "Jesus fucking Christ!" The idea of that particular abomination made her laugh sharply. Let Ella come up with a theological explanation for that! Caroline halted and flipped around to stare. The knees of her leggings had already collected round patches of dust. "Oh Caroline, I was just being silly," Margie said. "You'll have to learn to ignore me."

The baby looked doubtful.

"Go ahead. Keep going, you're doing great! Daddy will be so proud."

The baby went back to work and Margie crept to the door. But she couldn't bring herself to disappear without saying something; she hated seeing children manipulated in that way, as if they could be tricked out of their feelings. "I'm just going to go say good-bye to Grammie," she called out.

Caroline was so absorbed that she didn't even turn

around, but no sooner had Margie resumed her conversation than the baby began to cry, a plaintive cry that pinched Margie's stomach. "I have to go now, Mother," she said.

"But I'm so interested in what you have to say!"

"Oh—" She peered in the direction of the wailing, her nerves nearly shot. "Okay. I'll call you back."

"How soon? I have to go out in a little while," Ella said.

"Wait," Margie said anxiously. "Just hold on for a moment." She ran to the kitchen door and banged her shoulder against it; but rather than giving way and squeaking along on its familiar arc, the slab was stiff and unyielding and she smashed into it and gasped. After a moment she tried again, inching the door open gently until she hit the obstacle; there was a dull thud on contact.

"Caroline? Caroline?"

She listened, deeply sickened, blaming her ugliest traits—competitiveness, envy, superiority, inferiority, shrill egoism—for all of this. She was on the verge of a raw hysteria when the baby let out a chilling shriek, which she instinctively echoed, clamoring with fear and empathy. Together they screamed back and forth, filling the house with a chorus of forsaken wailing that sounded to Ella on her end of the line as though they'd turned on the television and were watching some jazzy police or hospital soap opera that had made them forget about her completely.

That wasn't very nice, she thought, and reflected how glad she would be when Margie's early-motherhood stage of tunnel vision came to an end. Until then, it was hardly worth calling. She sighed and hung up, then made a few quick scribbles about her latest notions so they could pick up where they left off when Margie wasn't so preoccupied.

The Tower

I WAS a bachelor, unto myself and complete. I'd never married or even fallen in love. I suppose I could blame my parents for not setting a very attractive example in the department of family affairs, but the same goes for most people and yet they hurl themselves into the domestic maelstrom; so I can't persuasively use that excuse. Anyway, it isn't true.

As a baby I already showed an inclination toward detachment. There were all sorts of family stories that showcased my early independence. I believed it was my nature, but later in life, women—frustrated, angry women—pointed out to me that perhaps my parents were glad to have a child who didn't ask much of them. Had I ever considered that they praised my self-sufficiency not because they honestly admired it, but so they could ignore me?

Your parents fucked you up, these women said; they then moved on to men who might be fucked up in different ways but could at least make a commitment.

Over time, I'd learned to recognize that type in an instant and save us both some unpleasant moments by steering clear. Clara Barnes was the kind of person I did best with, someone who could let the sexual phase of the relationship peter out naturally and ease into being buddies with no psychoanalytic lecture in between. She also had the rare attribute of looking nicer than she was, which went a long way toward making her interesting. We'd had our moment, and now we palled around amicably. It wasn't out of the question that we'd end up in the same bed again, but for the time being our fun consisted mainly of talking on the phone or in restaurants, comparing adventures.

On this particular day, she had a plan; she wanted me to drive her and two friends out to Montclair, New Jersey, to hear the Metropolitan Opera sing in a park.

"Please?" At forty, she still wheedled like a young girl. "I'll bring a picnic and pay for the tolls."

I was at my desk at the bank and glanced at my agenda. The evening was free. "I have season tickets. Good seats. In the opera house," I teased. "Why would I want to sit on the ground next to people who will probably be eating fried chicken from a bucket?"

"Don't be a snob, Edmund. The park was designed by Frederick Law Olmsted, so you can dwell on the lay of the land if you don't want to scope out the natives," she enticed. "Plus, I'm bringing a little treat for you."

"Oh?" Clara had the instincts of a madam, if not the discipline. "And what's its name?"

"Robin Blake. She works at the gallery where I filled

in last month. She's a hottie. And not a model. *And* she has no aspirations to act."

Like most of the women I saw, Clara had been both a model and an actress before making the ultimate career move of marrying rich. It didn't last, of course; and as she'd signed a prenup (believing it would never apply to *her*), she found herself at thirty-six in a one-bedroom on East Seventy-second (far east), doing odd jobs for friends and pinching pennies as she looked for *numero deux*. "Hmm," I stalled, playing hard-to-get, although I'd already decided I'd go.

"Come on, don't be an old fuddy-duddy."

I bristled. The last time I'd been to the doctor he'd referred to me as "middle-aged." I'd proved him wrong in varied ways since then, but the label had rattled me.

"I'll supply a picnic from Dean & DeLuca," she added.

"Hmm," I stalled. "I'm beginning to form a picture. You're willing to spend money, so there must be something—or someone—in it for you."

"No shit, Sherlock. Please?"

"This Robin sounds suspiciously down to earth. Are you sure I'll like her?"

"No, I'm not sure, but you've gone through all the models in town. You're going to have to expand your horizons."

"All right," I said. "But she'd better not be too serious. And your fellow better be worth it."

"What have we got to lose?" she said.

After we hung up I went to the bathroom and examined my waist in the mirror. Middle-aged, schmiddle-aged. I was trim as a marine.

"So I hear from Clara that we have something in common," I said to Robin Blake. "We're both going to be in Italy next month. Have you ever been?"

She shook her head.

"I go often. I have a lot of friends in various places. I love Italy."

She nodded, polite but unforthcoming. She appeared to be around twenty-five and had looks as advertised—brown hair, blue eyes, fine skin—but not much else I could discern. She'd been quiet on the drive out from the city, huddled in the back seat staring out the window, although not morose. She'd said she didn't much like to talk in cars.

We'd spread a blanket on the damp ground of Brookdale—which was no Central Park, but pretty enough on a breezy July night—and I was trying to draw her out, an exercise in tooth pulling that strained my deepest beliefs in good manners. Clara was having better luck. Her boy (I doubted he'd even made it through college yet) had one of Clara's feet in his lap and was massaging her toes. An image of her in an even more intimate posture came to mind, and I felt an atavistic twitch of jealousy thinking of this tight-limbed boy on the blanket being the next to see her that way. But as I had no better alternative to offer, I behaved myself and remained friendly to everyone.

"Where are you going, exactly?" I asked Robin.

She'd have to answer that, or so I thought. But she looked stricken.

"Why do you want to know?"

"If you think I'm going to track you down and make a pest of myself, that's not what I had in mind. I'm trying to make conversation."

She looked up at me from under a curtain of shining hair. "I'm sorry."

"You should be." I was genuinely angry.

"It's just that I've had some weird experiences." She fiddled with the straps of her sandals. She had nice feet, I had to give her that. Usually I hate bare feet. "You think that when men look at you and try to talk to you that they want to know what you're like, but a lot of them don't, not really. And it always takes me by surprise, because to me, I'm just myself. I don't think of my outside as disconnected from my inside. I think when someone talks to me and pays attention that . . . well. I sound naive, don't I?"

"There are worse things."

"You think?"

"Therefore I am." Ugh, I thought, but Robin smiled and began to recite.

> "I think therefore I am, I think,
>   Therefore I am I think,
> Therefore I think, I think I think,
>   Now let's go get a drink!"

I laughed. "What's that from?"

"Me. I turned it in as a philosophy paper. The teacher gave me an A, saying it was an excellent dialogue with Descartes. Not that I would want to talk to him. He believed animals have no feelings."

"Bastard!"

Robin nodded. I made an exaggeratedly disapproving face and she giggled; so I raised my eyebrows and she giggled some more, now with her hand over her mouth. We continued with this pantomime for a minute or so, with her egging me on by looking lovely as she laughed at my efforts. I didn't know women who behaved as if they were . . . happy. Clara and her ilk generally acted as though the only reason they walked the earth was because they didn't want to be caught dead in the cliché of a suicide. In contrast to all those louche ladies, Robin's silliness refreshed.

I entertained her well beyond my usual threshold of self-consciousness—I've often been glad I never had children because I'd no doubt embarrass myself around them—but it was fun to be delighting her. Her expression of simple pleasure was as intelligent as anything I'd come across in quite some time. The word *childlike* came to mind, but that was a lazy analysis. Her keenness bespoke maturity. She'd been distrustful of me only moments earlier, leery in an adult way.

"I'm mainly going to Porto Ercole," she said. "My mother has a house there."

"That's one of my favorite places on the planet."

"You're kidding! You've been there?"

I nodded, enjoying our sudden camaraderie.

"What's it like?" she asked.

"You've never been?" Hadn't she just said her mother lived there?

"I'd never heard of it until a few weeks ago."

Again, I wondered how this could be, but it was none of my business. "Oh, you'll adore it. It's a perfect combination of fishing villages and multimillionaires mimicking the simple life—Italy's answer to Tahiti, I call it. Lucky you!"

She searched my eyes as I spoke, as if to see beyond my words to the island itself, or at least to what I knew of it. For a moment she appeared transported, and I felt a surge of excitement at having moved her. However, before I could pursue this new pleasure, she dropped her gaze and began to pluck at the grass.

"So you think good people are attracted to the place?" she asked.

I said, lamely, that there were good and bad people everywhere.

"And many more who fall somewhere in between," I added. "That's my stab at philosophy for the day."

"I suppose," she said.

She looked away.

"Where on the island is your mother?" I wanted to get the conversation back on track.

"I don't know. *Torre* something."

I told her there were old Sienese watchtowers all

along the coast, that I remembered some on the island, and that they were often quite elegant. From the road you saw a ruin, but inside you were apt to be bombarded with modernity, sleek spatial ideas and tomorrow's furniture. The watchtowers had been discovered, in other words.

"What hasn't," Robin said. There was a wistfulness to her tone that was both regretful and resigned—just the right response, I thought, which of course meant it matched my feelings on the subject. I was beginning to think Clara really did have my number. As if sensing her appearance in my thoughts, Clara elbowed me and announced she was hungry. She looked at each of us avidly, and we turned away from our private conversation to unpack the old carpetbag full of food she'd brought.

Robin was different yet again during the meal, light and funny. She asked Clara's fellow—I never registered his name—if she could have the morsel of food that he was on the verge of putting in his mouth. It was as though she instinctively knew how to reveal him—I supposed Clara had asked her to check him out—and he came out well in the instance, showing no sign of hesitation before he gently turned the fork in Robin's direction. We clapped at his chivalry, and he, getting the joke, offered his plate to each of us in turn. Clara beamed; she was proud of him, and of herself for picking him. I, in turn, thrummed with adrenaline whenever I looked at Robin.

We could have talked quietly during the opera—we
were outside—but all four of us drew back once the
music began, each for our own reasons. Robin seemed to
be genuinely interested. Clara, I guessed, had depleted
her tanks by making such an effort—feeding the multi-
tudes, et cetera—and needed to refuel. Meanwhile her
boy appeared to be under the sway of middlebrow con-
cert hall manners, silence denoting respect. I could picture him being moved by a Whitney Houston rendition
of the national anthem sung in a ballpark.

As for myself, I had my own reason for keeping quiet.
The language that might explain how I felt eluded me
while everything else that crossed my mind seemed
trivial. What was happening? My stomach was a wreck.
The opera was half over before I understood that I was
in the grip of a common condition, the same state of
mind that inspired the libretto soaring from the stage
and that shone from many faces in the crowd around me.
I knew the word for it—Clara and I called it the ultimate four-letter word—but I'd never before uttered it
and had come to believe I couldn't. Yet as I snuck
glances at Robin, chin on knees, hair caped over her
shoulders, I began to think maybe that belief was due
to slip from my repertoire.

Around noon the next day, clearly as soon as she woke
up, Clara called to do the postmortems.

"So?"

"Now Clara," I warned.

"What? You're suddenly coy?"

"There's nothing to tell."

"Come on. I saw the way you were looking at each other."

"We talked. That's all."

"Well, then, have I got a story for you. You see, her mother—"

I cut her off. "Actually, she told me." We'd sat on the steps of her building and, under the yellow light from the sconces, Robin told me the woman in Italy was her birth mother, the trip a pilgrimage of sorts. Her adoptive parents had had children of their own shortly after they procured her, and she'd always felt like a "dry run" who didn't belong.

"Oh. That was quick. It took two weeks of standing around all day together in the gallery for her to tell me."

"Huh," I muttered noncommittally, not wanting to go there. Quickly, I changed to her favorite subject. "How about you? Did you have fun?"

There was a pause. I hadn't fooled her.

"Oh Edmund. Poor you," she sighed. "Well, I suppose it had to happen sometime. Call me when it blows over."

"Thanks, Clara. No offense, but in that case I hope I'll never call you again."

She laughed wickedly. In one night, I'd become a person who didn't enjoy that sound anymore.

I had two weeks with her, then only two days, and finally just an hour before she left. I hadn't yet put into words how I felt, though I believed I'd made it clear. For once I had a sense of future about a relationship and didn't want to rush. I knew she liked me, too, and hoped that when she'd satisfied herself about her mother her emotions would form a match for mine.

She was affectionate, and I was wildly attracted to her, but for once I wanted to wait. I was like a nineteenth-century suitor, excited, protective, curious. When I was with her I was funny and cool, but after our dates I walked for hours, trying to manage the crazy energy I got from being with her. I could barely concentrate at work; people kept asking me if anything was wrong. No, I told them firmly. Superstitiously, I didn't want to talk about it.

Once or twice I was tempted to phone Clara to see if she'd spoken to Robin and if Robin had said anything about me, but when I imagined her teasing and innuendoes it wasn't hard to resist making the call. Robin was my secret. I was content to keep it that way, even on the sleepless nights when I normally would have riffled my address books for numbers of accommodating friends. Now I didn't need the distraction of company; I was no longer alone.

I'd considered taking my vacation earlier than planned and going with her but, close as we were becoming, even the suggestion seemed like an intrusion unless it came from her. I'm sure she thought of it, too— she thought of everything. But she never mentioned it, so the possibility shrank and shrank until it disappeared. Now there was no time left to make that kind of arrangement, and she was not the type to suggest an impossible possibility for the sake of heightening the drama of the farewell. She'd packed the day before while I was at the office. There was nothing left to do.

"Walk me to a cab. I'd like to get to the airport early."

It was a steamy morning and I grew clammy as I carried her bag up the block. (I adored her for taking only one, and a small one at that.) Broadway was thronged with the early-to-work crowd and old women out to do their shopping before the heat became unbearable. The day smelled of urine and orange rinds and gasoline, and it would only grow worse. But I had my office to go to. I could look forward to climate control, and the hush of muffling carpets.

"I'll write," she said.

"Please do." She hadn't given me her address, and I knew that was a purposeful decision on her part. She'd get in touch when she was ready; I was sure of it. "I'll see you in a few weeks."

She leaned her forehead against my chest and clutched my lapels. I realized I'd always wanted a girl to do that.

"I wish we had more time," she said.

"We will."

Her cab pulled away. I waved. I was nauseous, aching, but it felt good.

It's odd, the roles and identities one takes for oneself, especially the lesser ones, the ones of which we aren't even conscious until they're threatened. Since adolescence I've thought of myself as a good traveler, a person who not only knows the layouts of dozens of airports and the concierges at dozens of hotels, but also can pass the time with equanimity, no matter what. I can lie on the filthiest terminal floor and sleep like a babe. But on that flight to Italy, I was as restless as a six-year-old. Are we there yet? How much longer will it be? I paced the aisles, maniacally switched channels on the headset, shifted in my seat. Thank God there were a lot of cranky children on the plane to distract everyone from my behavior. I probably seemed like just another hyper businessman.

Every so often I reread the one and only letter she'd sent. It was brief, but it said, albeit subtly, all the right things—at least as far as her feelings for me were concerned. On her end, the trip had been weird. When she arrived at the watchtower, she discovered her mother had gone off on a business trip, leaving behind no itinerary, no phone number, no date of return. Robin suspected she was being given the brush-off, but the housekeepers assured her otherwise, so she decided to stay on at the *torre* for a while and wait for her mother to reappear. It was all very odd. Robin sounded as though she was making the best of it, but the situation still bugged me—selfishly, I'd hoped she'd have it all sorted out by the time *I* arrived. I'd never tested how much gentlemanliness I had in me, but I suspected I'd just about used it up. Luckily, she'd kept her phone and address a mystery; otherwise I might have barraged her day and night. *I have to see this through on my own*, she'd written—which gave me strength.

Finally, touchdown. I looked for her at the gate even though I knew she wouldn't be there; I'd decided to surprise her rather than have her come down to Rome alone. A rented car, a feverish, impatient drive up to the island. It wasn't until I arrived at the town square that I noticed what a perfect day it was, a clear, Mediterranean day, whitewashed and soft gold and blue.

I was on the verge of asking directions to all the watchtowers on the island when I spotted her. It seemed a good omen; I couldn't wait another minute and a sympathetic god had taken pity and brought her near. I've heard women remark, upon seeing their children across the neutral expanse of a room, how very little the creatures looked in contrast to when they were close and loomed large, their stature commensurate with their importance rather than their size. I had this same sense now. For the past few weeks Robin had eclipsed everything else in my life. I hadn't been able to see past her. Now here she was, a pretty American girl in a white polo shirt and seersucker pants, arms tan, hair pinned up with strands escaping, sipping a cappuccino in a town square on an Italian summer day. Doubtless there were hundreds like her all over Europe. It was absurd that I'd been so done in by her.

But of course I was. This particular American girl was the one who moved me.

"Is this seat free?" I asked, Cary Grantish.

She jumped up and hugged me. Then, the kiss I'd been imagining all night.

"I'm waiting for my mother," she joked when we finally sat down, "but I don't think she's coming, so you may sit here for now."

"Still no sign?"

Robin shook her head. "Nope. Can you believe it? But let's not talk about her. Tell me what you've been up to."

"Not much. Thinking about you, mostly."

"Goody!" She rubbed her hands together. I liked those hands.

A waiter materialized and I ordered a coffee. He made an assessment of us in the manner of waiters everywhere, like one of those caricaturists who sketch you in thirty seconds. This one, however, had European tact—I'd no idea what he thought. I'd gotten to the age when waiters either were apt to wink at me if I were with a girl, or to assume I was her father—neither being a compliment in my book. All right, Robin was young compared to me—but not *too* young. There was no need for me to feel defensive. One of the advantages of the solitary way I'd lived my life was that I owed no one an explanation or an apology.

"And you?" I asked. "Did you think about me?"

She frowned. "Didn't you get my letter?"

I nodded. I wanted to hear her say it, though. She understood.

"I missed you, Edmund. I've missed you all my life."

There was a pause while we sat quietly, soaking each other in.

"So what would you like to do?" I asked.

She thought for a moment. "Part of me wants to keep waiting, but another part thinks I'd be a chump to stay here another day. I mean, I'm being given a hint, and maybe I should take it."

I agreed. Her mother was in no rush to see her, that was for sure. I couldn't imagine any business taking so long, knowing she was waiting at home. "So shall we move on?"

"I couldn't impose on you."

"Hello? What do you think I'm doing here?"

She blushed, then giggled. "You have a point. All right. Let's go to the tower and I'll get my stuff."

"I made a reservation at a hotel in Siena."

"I can handle that," she said simply.

Now it was my turn to blush, or flush, or something like that—I got a definite buzz. Things were shaping up even better than I expected. I reached for my wallet so we could get going. As I was fishing out some money, I noticed Robin suddenly looked upset.

"What's wrong?" I asked.

"I see Nancy," she said. "Damn! I don't feel like talking to her right now."

I remembered Nancy was the housekeeper, or the social secretary—at any rate, one of the staff at the tower. I looked around, but before I could guess which person she was among the groups coming off the yachts for lunch, I spotted a different source of consternation. There, not fifty feet away, was Georgina Stokes—an old, old lover. I hadn't seen her in ages. In an instant I registered that she hadn't aged very well. She'd become one of those blowsy blondes who wears a face plastered with amazing makeup above a body swathed in tunics and stretch pants. Clara would be horrified. She'd taught me to notice how the heels on such women pooled over the edges of their sandals. My gaze dropped to Georgina's feet. Sure enough.

Then Georgina stared at me, too.

"Uh oh," Robin said. "She spotted us."

"Who?"

"Nancy."

"That's Nancy?" I tried to figure out what was going on but my brain crawled. Meanwhile Georgina headed off in the other direction. She looked as confused as I was.

"Yes. She's leaving, thank God."

Full of dread, I offered my information. "You won't believe this, but I know that woman. Not as Nancy, though. Her name is Georgina Stokes."

Robin stared at me. "Georgina Stokes is my birth mother."

I don't know who was the more stunned, me or Robin. For a moment neither of us could speak, or think, or do anything significant. The most we could manage was to watch Georgina jump on her Vespa and speed away.

We had to confront her, of course, or at least Robin did. I'd have preferred to run away, but knew better than to suggest it. From the square we drove back to the tower, and though we talked, we were each caught in private corners of fear and disgust.

"Why would she lie to me about who she is?" Robin wondered. "She doesn't even care about me enough to introduce herself."

"She's a selfish, childish person, always was," I said. "Not to put too fine a point on it."

She inhaled fiercely and struggled to find the bright side. "In a way, this is good, though, isn't it? I mean, you can tell me about her."

It wasn't good, though. The more I thought about it, the more awful it got. Eventually, as Robin settled down, she, too, saw the uglier possibilities.

"You didn't sleep with her, did you?" she asked.

She was wild now, anxious, on the verge of withdrawing altogether.

"It was a long time ago," I said.

After that, we didn't speak.

She went in alone to talk to Georgina while I waited in the car. Even as I made the worst calculations of my life, I couldn't help but notice the spectacular surroundings. The sea was dark, a true navy, the lawn thick with thyme and arugula. I found a chaise and, incredibly, fell asleep. My mind needed an escape, I suppose, and I hadn't slept during the flight or, for that matter, the past six weeks. When I awoke Georgina was standing over me, throwing a large, dank shadow.

"Well, well, well," she said. "I wasn't expecting you, Edmund. *Quel* surprise."

I leaped up. "Where's Robin?"

"Packing. She'll be right out."

She was barely rattled. I wanted to strangle her. "Whatever game you're playing here, Georgina, I don't want any part of it."

She dismissed my stance, her bracelets clanking. "Don't worry. It's all straightened out."

I clenched my teeth, waiting for an explanation.

"I never wanted children, Edmund. But by the time I figured out I was pregnant, it was too late to do anything about it. When Robin got in touch I was curious, but I got cold feet. My friend Nell is very jealous. She doesn't want to share me with anyone."

She smiled, both lascivious and triumphant. I supposed Nell was the other "housekeeper." It was typical of Georgina to think that a revelation about her being with a woman was the most shocking aspect of the situation. I wanted to get away from her as quickly as I could, so I got to the point.

"Was it me?" I asked. "Am I the father?"

She laughed. "Oh Edmund, you always were one to flatter yourself. The truth is, I don't know. I was popular in those days." She winked.

"You have no idea?" I couldn't remember ever hating anyone as much.

"You could take one of those tests if it bothers you. But why not just forget it? You two make a cute couple. It could easily be someone else. Why make problems for yourself?"

Why indeed?

"Robin has a right to know who her parents are, even if it's us," I said. To be honest, I didn't know I'd made any such decision, or if I even believed that. The words just came out.

She laughed. "I always thought you were a closet romantic."

I arranged for the tests through my doctor, but Robin went to the lab separately, having made it clear she didn't want us to see each other as we waited for the results. Three weeks, I was told it would take. *Three weeks*—what had I gotten us into? I'd pictured a minor delay, a minute or two, like one of those pregnancy tests on TV. I didn't think I could wait. Wouldn't it be easier and more sane for us to sweat it out together? I tried leaving a few sweet/amusing messages on her machine, but when that didn't work, there was nothing for me to do but to go back to the office and postpone my vacation, hoping we'd take one together when everything was settled. The city was hot and what passes for empty among people I know, which means parking spaces are easy to come by. I went from one air-conditioned space to the next, yet felt the heat always present and vaguely menacing. Italy was just as hot; I knew that. But it wasn't the same. So much for summer fun. The best that can be said is that I lived through those weeks, all the while supposing that afterward I'd feel I could live through anything.

For whatever that was worth.

I hadn't the heart to contact what few of my friends were around, so I spent whatever time I couldn't manage to kill wondering how I'd behave if it turned out I was her father. How could I possibly watch her go out with other men and pretend to be anything but sick about it? There were many moments when I cursed Georgina for advising the easy way out. I might well have taken it if I could have dissociated it from her. I didn't want to be noble, or to do the right thing. And Georgina was probably right, I thought; chances were it wasn't me, and I was making problems even raising the possibility. I couldn't even remember if I was with her at exactly the right time; we were casual, and on and off for ages. The more I thought about it, the more I was sure I was in the clear. Wouldn't I feel some sense of taboo if we were related? I didn't. I still wanted Robin, all of her, all to myself.

I'm not the father, I repeated over and over; it's not me, it's not me, it's not me.

Finally the doctor called. Of course I knew it had nothing to do with my will, my mantra, my anything. It was a roll of the dice, and I got lucky. But to me, it felt miraculous, like at last I got my wish.

She wanted to hear the results in person, so we met at a Starbucks and settled into a pair of velvet club chairs. The king and queen, I thought. Happily.

"Coffee?" I offered. She looked so pretty in her short-sleeved lime green sweater set. Thin, though.

"Just tell me," she said.

"Okay—"

She held up her hand. "No, wait. I have something to say first."

I nodded agreeably. It's easy to postpone good news.

"Darn. I had a whole speech I wanted to deliver, and now I can't remember it."

She gave me a beseeching glance as if I might be able to help.

"Maybe I should just go ahead," I said.

"Not yet—I remember now. I wanted to say that no matter what, I appreciate the support you've given me this summer. Having you to think about really helped when I was languishing in that tower all by myself."

She paused to see if I understood her implication. I let her know, yes, it was a relief we hadn't had to wonder, on top of everything else, whether or not we'd committed incest.

"I haven't given you much in return," she went on.

"Hopefully in the future I'll have the chance." She noticed how close I was to bursting and leaned forward preemptively, to deliver the coup de grâce. "So no matter what happens, I want us to always be friends."

I grinned. "But we don't have to be."

She crinkled her brow.

"We don't have to be friends, because I'm not your father. We can be—everything."

I was ready to grab her and make a dash for city hall, then carry her over a threshold somewhere. I was nuts, delirious—but she was silent. I thought perhaps she needed a moment to let it all sink in. A moment passed, though, and she did no more than lay her hands on the table, then pull them back into her lap again.

"Hey," I said eventually. "Knock knock. Anyone there?"

She shrank deeper into the chair. "You didn't want to be my father?"

A curve ball. Stupid of me, I suppose, but it had never crossed my mind that she might be looking for that outcome. For the first time since we sat down I was aware of our surroundings. I noticed voices, chairs scraping, clattering behind the espresso bar. It was a shock to realize we hadn't been having the same dream lately. I began to fall back to earth and stiffened in anticipation of a crash.

"I'd be honored to be your father," I said, "but I was hoping for something more."

"What's a deeper commitment than parenthood? What could ever be more than that?"

She looked unbearably sad. Orphaned.

"I want to marry you," I said, although I sensed it was useless. I doubt if the phrase was ever spoken as woefully. I wasn't surprised to see her shake her head.

"You slept with my mother, Edmund."

"Robin, that was years ago. Decades."

"I know, but—" She began to cry. I fetched a napkin and she clutched it absentmindedly as the tears fell on her sweater.

"This is crazy," I said. "You're willing to throw away everything we have between us because I hung out with Georgina Stokes in the seventies?"

"I still want to be friends." It came out piecemeal, between sobs.

"I have friends." I got up to leave but hovered, hoping she'd relent, until my pride took over and marched me out the door.

On the next block I stopped abruptly. It occurred to me that I was walking into the rest of my life, and that the direction I was taking was rather bleak. Did I really want to not know her anymore, not see that face? I couldn't imagine it. But I'd have to set her straight that I wasn't eager to be a father figure. I'd tell her I wasn't going to give up hope that she'd change her mind. I'd set limits, be clear, let her know exactly what I was all about. She was just walking out the door when I caught up with her.

"All right, all right, all right," I said, throwing up my arms both literally and figuratively.

She smiled a teary smile.

And so we began again.

A few weeks later I ran into Clara near MOMA. She looked great, glowing and relaxed.

"Did you hear?" she asked. "I'm getting hitched again."

"Congratulations!"

"Edmund," she elbowed me, "you know you're not supposed to say that to the woman. Only the man gets congratulated."

"So whom should I applaud?"

She gave the name of a man I knew, a quiet guy who collected model trains. I'd never have imagined the two of them together, but then again, I was no authority on who belonged with whom.

"And you?" she asked. "Are you still seeing Robin Blake?"

"Not in the way you think."

"So it didn't work out."

"I wouldn't say that exactly."

"But you're available?"

"I suppose . . ."

"Good!"

She began to tell me about various events preceding her wedding for which she'd need extra men, but I didn't pay much attention. Instead, I was thinking about how I really was ready for anything after the summer's debacle, whether it be feeling genuinely glad for Clara, or getting to know Robin without expectations, or finally slowing down enough to think about all I'd missed by being so *independent* and what I might do to make up for it.

"So give me a buzz," Clara said.

I feigned shock. "Clara! You're an engaged woman!"

She laughed, then sighed. "I do want this marriage to work. I love him, Edmund. I feel really alive, maybe for the first time ever."

"I love, therefore I am?"

"Something like that. Strange, isn't it?"

I shrugged. "Stranger things have happened," I said, and wished her all the best.

The Secret Spot

IT WAS *her*, no doubt about it. She stood just below
Helen on a steep brushy hill in Central Park—Straw-
berry Fields, to be exact—tucking errant shirttails into
the waistband of the boy with whom Helen's own son,
Evan, had been playing for the last twenty minutes.
Helen could only see the woman's forehead (seamless)
and the tip of her nose (ski jump), but she was sure it
was Julia, *the* Julia, the woman who'd tried to snake
Nick away from her while Helen was busy being pregnant and her guard was down.

Now she'd taken Helen by surprise—again—and
Helen had to hold back a scream as her heart pinched
for a beat. Calm down, she soothed herself. It's okay.
You know what to do. You're in control.

She'd been waiting five years for this encounter,
scripting and planning for it, but it was crucial that
none of that showed. She needed to be the picture of
serenity and innocence for her scheme to work; she
must behave as though her stomach was the calmest
surface of a summer pond, and Julia the most casual of
acquaintances. She set to work nudging her features

into a mask of composure as she assessed Julia's battle readiness.

Helen remembered her as being elegant in a spare American-schoolgirl way, an impression borne out now by how the sleeves of Julia's taupe cardigan dangled aristocratically from her shoulders and the toes of her piped leather shoes pressed with entitlement into the newly seeded grass. She looked prepared for nothing more strenuous than a brunch at Tavern on the Green, or more mentally taxing than whatever was the big box office movie at Loews 84th. I could take her with my eyes shut, Helen concluded—except that she wanted to see Julia writhe.

She took a breath and began the conversation. "Hello."

Julia finished her grooming and laid her hands on her boy's shoulders. "These two monkeys seem to be getting along, don't they?" she said. "It's so easy for children to make friends."

She shifted to see to whom she was speaking, shading her eyes against the bright afternoon sun. Helen saw the exact moment of recognition; Julia cocked her head. Be friendly, Helen reminded herself. She smiled, and Julia managed a smile back. Perfect. Julia was on the defensive already, with not a word exchanged. Just as Helen had planned.

"Julia Davis?" Helen boomed. "Is that you?"

Both boys looked up curiously, too much so for their age—Julia's child appeared to be five-and-something, like Evan—and Helen knew she was overdoing it. "I haven't seen you in years," she said in a far more controlled manner. Yes, that was better. The boys had lost interest and were mugging at each other again.

"I'm sorry, I've forgotten your name," Julia said.

Sure you have, Helen thought. She bristled at the insult even as she admired the gambit. What better putdown than to pretend a hated face had been expunged from the memory? Points to Julia, who was perhaps more up to a skirmish than she was willing to show. Helen felt a surge of exhilaration. A victory would be even more satisfying coming out of an even match.

"I'm Helen Hall. Nick's wife. Remember? We had dinner together one night at the Popover Cafe?"

Julia feigned a trip to the memory bank, brow furrowed, then bloomed with apparent recollection. "Oh, Helen! Hello, and forgive me—the sun was in my eyes."

"I have an urge to say 'fancy meeting you here,' but this *is* Central Park—although Nick and I have always thought of this particular spot as our secret. It's where we got engaged." There. The first volley had gone off easily, and by the look of Julia's widening eyes, a point was scored.

"Oh, I like that," she said. "Where we go in Maine you always have to walk through miles of forest or pick over a stretch of abandoned coast before you get to someone's secret spot. Then it turns out to be nothing more than a view or a mushroom bog or a blackberry bramble. It's never as earth-shattering as people think—but the way they guard it!" She shrugged at the way people were. "I like your idea, though—a public secret spot. That's really good."

As if Helen had asked for Julia's approval! She fought the sensation of offense that curled her hands into fists. Think like a lawyer, she told herself. Ask questions to which you know the answer. "You live around here, don't you?" Twenty-six West Seventy-fourth, to be exact. Julia's was the first information Helen looked up each year when the new Manhattan phone book came out.

"Yes, I'm still in the same place."

Julia's eyes darted around, and Helen realized she was scouting for Nick. How dare she even think of him? She was thrilled to be able to quash any hopes Julia might have of a reunion.

"We moved to Irvington. We just came in for the day. Poor Nick had to go to the office for a while, but we're meeting him later."

"Oh. Great."

Relief, Helen surmised. She's relieved not to have to see Nick with his family; she thinks she's off the hook. Little did Julia know that that would actually have been the lesser struggle; Helen wouldn't have had as much room to maneuver in front of Nick.

"I've heard Irvington is nice," Julia said.

"We like it. But we miss the city. Nick comes in to work, but I only get in every couple of weeks. I have to admit that the city does seem much more glamorous when you're not dealing with the day-to-day inconveniences. It's like an affair versus a marriage—but that's not reality, is it?" She paused to emphasize the comparison. "Sometimes I meet Nick for dinner, and then we spend the night at the Stanhope. It's all very romantic. . Although I'm sure it probably sounds suburban and dull to you." Excellent!

"No, I grew up in Wynnemoor, outside of—"

Helen rushed to cut her off, hoping to avoid another distracting monologue like the one on Maine. "And is this gorgeous creature yours?"

Julia nodded and fiddled with his bangs, a standard gesture of maternal pride. Well, she's entitled to that, Helen thought. The boy was adorable.

"This is Peter," Julia said.

On his own, the boy shook Helen's hand.

"Good God," Helen exclaimed, "a boy with manners! I can only imagine the torture you must have inflicted to get him to do that."

Julia's eyes widened and then flicked from side to side, as if she wasn't sure she understood what had just been said and was looking for someone who did. Helen noted her confusion with satisfaction. As she was the only other adult present, it was up to her to be of help. Solicitously, she touched Julia's arm. "Oh, I'm teasing, I think it's wonderful. And this is our son, Evan."

Helen nudged him and he looked up, squinting. Julia automatically shifted her position until she was between him and the sun; he basked in the subtle consideration. "Hello, Evan," she said, her tone neither cute nor studied. She behaved naturally, in other words—although it was clear to Helen that Julia displayed an unnatural interest in him. Was it possible that she still carried a torch for Nick to the degree that she might glean some satisfaction from seeing him reconfigured in his son?

For the first time ever Helen found herself wishing that Evan had inherited a greater proportion of Nick's good looks, and then felt flustered by the betrayal in that notion. She'd only meant she'd want him different to further torment Julia. Evan was absolutely perfect as he was. She told herself that it was always disconcerting to see a child—a human being—as beautiful as Peter. As she'd watched him and Evan play on the rocks she'd found her gaze shifting between her customary vigilance for Evan's safety to an objective marveling at Peter's looks. For a while she'd thought she recognized him—could Evan have played with him when they were little? She'd decided he appeared familiar to her in the way that people in the city had all become familiar during the years she lived there, until they seemed like a mass of former friends and acquaintances. She'd thoroughly admired him when she hadn't known who he was—and was bemused by the irony that he was Julia's. How solicitous of Julia to provide yet another reason to resent her!

"I was wondering where his parents were," Helen said.

Julia stiffened. "I was just on the bench, reading. I could see—"

"Oh, you lucky woman! I haven't found the time to read a book since Evan was born. I'm old-fashioned, I guess, and don't dare take my eyes off him when he's in a public park. I think it's wonderful that you can be so casual."

"I watch Peter, I—"

"He's gorgeous, really stunning. I should think you'd have to be extra careful with a boy like him."

"I am," Julia mustered, but she was shaken and groped for Peter in a manner that told Helen she was about to flee. Quickly Helen bent to the children.

"Why don't you boys go off and play some more while we mothers have a chat?"

Hopefully, Peter looked at Julia.

"We really should go," she said.

"Do you have to? It's a shame to cheat the children out of their fun," Helen said. This was easy sailing. As she'd hoped, there was a pause, with all eyes on Julia.

"All right," she caved, "but only for a little while."

The boys were back on the rocks in seconds, and Julia was obeying Helen's "suggestion" that they sit down and get comfortable. Helen led them to a flat rock nearby and settled herself firmly—she was going nowhere soon. She looked off toward Central Park West and ran through the lines she'd so carefully crafted and rehearsed over the years. Then she locked Julia into her sights.

"I've thought about you, you see," she began. "I liked you so much that night we met that I hoped we'd continue to see each other, and maybe be friends."

There!

"Really? You never called me."

There was a pause. Helen hadn't expected Julia to challenge her false claim, but she could handle it. "I was too shy," she said, pleased with herself for thinking so quickly. "But no, I remember clearly, when Nick and I were lying in bed that night"—picture that, she thought—"we talked about you and I told him how much I liked you. I suggested the four of us go away together for a weekend. Oh, are you cold? You've got goosebumps."

"Mmm." Julia threaded her arms into her sleeves.

"Most women seem to get hotter after they have children," Helen said. "You really are different from other mothers, aren't you? Oh well." She shrugged and there was a spate of silence—planned for—during which she prayed Julia was imagining the four of them going away for the weekend together and squirming at the thought of it. Squirm she should—a vision of hell was what it was. What would she and Julia's husband have done while Julia and Nick tried and failed to avoid staring at each other? Scrabble? Parcheesi? A fling of their own?

After that dinner she'd had a number of choice words in her mind for Julia all right, but none of them were repeatable. She shuddered, remembering.

"Now you're cold, too," Julia said.

Helen bristled. Was Julia needling her back? Helen couldn't be sure. She could hardly say why she was trembling, but she hated to allow the misinterpretation to stand. She saw no other choice, however. She nodded, reminding herself it was a means to an end.

"It's usually broiling on my birthday," she said, side-stepping a clarification.

"Today's your birthday? Happy birthday."

"Thank you."

"Is that why you're in the city? To celebrate?"

Helen nodded. "We're going to dinner and the ballet."

"Nice. Peter likes the ballet, too. He doesn't yet know he's not supposed to—that it's a girl thing, I mean. I hope he can resist that pressure."

Again Helen tuned her radar to pick up evidence of sarcasm, but it was beyond her detection if it was there at all. She wondered if she'd been wrong before, when she'd thought Julia was playing her. It didn't really matter either way—as long as she got her digs in. "Yes, it's part of my birthday present. Nick's such a sweetheart. As a matter of fact . . ."

She broke off to register a sudden inspiration. It was all she could do not to yelp with delight. For all the times she'd imagined a dialogue with Julia, never in her wildest fantasies could she have thought up the stagy bit of business she was about to enact. It was too perfect. The gods were on her side. Happy birthday indeed.

She tossed the lure. "Since you know Nick, you'll appreciate this."

"Oh, I haven't spoken to him for years . . ." Julia protested.

Helen waved this disclaimer away and pulled the card from her bag. He'd slipped it in without her knowing; she'd discovered it when she and Evan were preparing to leave the house and she'd read it on the train. "Go ahead. Have a look." She steered it into Julia's hand.

"Oh no, I couldn't. I don't have my glasses." Julia dropped it as if it were hot.

"All right, I'll read it to you." She glanced up at Julia and saw pure misery, which she alchemized for her own consumption as glee.

"Dear Helen," she read in a clear, inflated tone. "My birthday present to you this year is part selfish. I would like for us to have another little one. So how about we go to Bermuda to try? I love you, Nick."

When she'd finished she gave a wistful sigh that suggested—she hoped—all the romance of a wonderful marriage and, in the spirit of sharing her wealth—ha!—she proffered the card to Julia with the handwriting showing. Julia took it this time, feigning politeness, but there was a telltale moment when her thumb strayed to touch the handwriting. Finally she handed it back, and Helen made a show of replacing it in its envelope and then tucking it firmly in her bag. He's mine, all mine, her gestures proclaimed, and Julia acknowledged the fact by wilting even further and digging her nails into her palms.

This *is* fun, Helen thought—and reminded herself, to

dispel the twinge of guilt she felt for gloating, that she deserved any pleasure she could get out of it. It had been a long time after she found out about Julia's designs on Nick before she could conceive of any kind of pleasure at all, a couple of years at least before her imagined encounters with Julia consisted of much more than a series of furious questions. How could you? What kind of a person are you, anyway? Didn't it weigh on you at all that I was pregnant?

At least she was fairly sure that nothing had actually happened between the two of them; it frightened her to consider what she might have done if it had, what murderous depths she'd have located in herself in that event when what little had occurred had been enough to shatter her.

Sometimes she thought it would have been better if she'd never found the letter, if she'd remained innocent. It wasn't difficult to talk herself out of that wistful mood, however, as she believed it was always preferable to know the facts. Facts were the foot soldiers in a campaign—you couldn't win a war without them—and the fact was that she'd found the letter Nick had written Julia, had copied it before replacing it in his drawer, and had subsequently committed it to memory. The next time she checked, the letter was gone; mailed, presumably. But she had it in her mind, permanently engraved right next to the Twenty-third Psalm, "The Land of Counterpane," and various other essentials she'd learned over the years. She couldn't begin to count the number of times she'd recited it to herself; she ran through it again now.

Dear Julia, Although I'm moved that you would reveal your feelings to me, I have to tell you that I cannot fulfill the role you'd like me to play in your life. My own feelings—and scruples—prevent me from doing what you suggest. I will take this chance, though, to say I think you are an incredible person, and deserve much love and happiness. But we cannot see each other anymore. I hope you'll understand. Nick.

Even after all these years, it gave her chills. She still found herself cheering at the part where Nick wrote he couldn't see Julia anymore. She must have smiled at the thought, for the next thing she knew Julia was smiling back at her and lifting her eyebrows slightly in a mute appeal to be let in on the fun.

"So you *do* want another child!" Julia announced.

Helen was caught off-guard—there was a price to be paid for deviating from the script, no matter how clever it seemed to be to do so—but she quickly regrouped and went to work determining the content of the next salvo. Under normal circumstances, that wouldn't at all have been a personal question. Helen had observed that women found the same kind of common ground in discussions of pregnancy and childbirth that men did in talk of sports. Another child for Helen, however, meant another child with Nick, which loaded the question considerably. How could Julia possibly be interested in an answer—any answer? She was making this almost too easy.

"I wouldn't mind trying for one," Helen said suggestively. "Nick's such a good father, too. That certainly makes it more tempting," she added.

"That's nice. Lucky for all of you."

Helen shook her head. "No, not luck. We've made our commitments—the rest is all follow-through." She paused. "Although perhaps it would be fair to say that we are lucky our adherence to our values makes us happy." She settled back to wait for this last claim to settle—it was one of the sentences she'd planned—but she could see she wasn't hitting her target squarely enough. Julia looked pensive rather than pained.

"So how about you?" Helen groped.

Julia shrugged. "Another child, you mean? I'd love to but . . . I can't right now. Maybe someday."

"Why can't you?" Helen made herself sound concerned. This was nosy, yes, but Julia was an adult. She could decide whether or not she wanted to answer.

"Well, the last I heard, you need a man for that!" She laughed the way women are apt to when telling strangers about their worst misfortunes. When Helen didn't laugh along, but instead looked honestly confused, Julia's hands flew to her cheeks. "Oh, you don't know, do you. But how could you know?" She shook her head, then brought her hands back down to her lap and laced her fingers. "I'm divorced."

"You are?"

Julia nodded. Helen couldn't help but show her honest surprise.

"I am. I have been since very soon after I met you. You see—"

She paused and took a long look out across the park, just as Helen had done earlier when she ran through her script. She appeared to be weighing options, what to admit, what to suppress—or perhaps she, too, had ready-made lines she was trying to remember? Helen began to shake her head in disbelief—the woman had nerve—and then disguised the disapproving gesture by craning to check on the boys, who appeared occupied, safe, and content. She envied them for their obliviousness, for how they lived in the present. It was painful to think she'd carried the burden of Julia for longer than they'd been alive. They'd just hunched down over something, a bug or a flower, bare knees gleaming, when Julia spoke again.

"It was simple, really. I fell in love with someone else."

Helen's heart stopped cold. Nick had never told her anything about what went on between him and Julia, and in spite of constant temptation, she'd never asked. She'd considered doing so, of course, but doubted she could pull it off without her anger flaring, which would give the whole subject more gravitas than she wanted to admit it deserved. Yet she longed to know. She doubted anything could be worse than her imagination. She sat on her hands and in her mind rehearsed her voice. After a moment, she felt ready. "I see. And your husband found out about it?"

Julia lifted her face. She was silent for another moment, then smiled to herself. "No, I told him. I know that sounds stupid. I even think it sounds foolish sometimes. But I didn't want to live with secrets." She shook her head, as if amazed at herself. "It wasn't as though I was looking to meet someone. I couldn't stop it, though, once it began. It was like nothing I'd ever experienced before. I was a crazy person—or completely sane for the first time, depending on your opinion about those kinds of things. I felt both, I guess. I got completely carried away, but that seemed exactly right. Does that make any sense to you?"

Helen avoided her eyes, her invitation. "How did the man feel?"

"The same. Or I thought he did." She touched her fingers to her lips and was far away, suddenly.

"But he didn't?" she prompted.

"What?"

Earth to Julia, Helen thought impatiently.

"He didn't love you."

"No."

She hung her head despondently and Helen almost felt sorry for her—but not quite. "Didn't you feel guilty about it?"

"Terribly. That's why I told."

"I mean, didn't you feel guilty toward the man's wife?"

In the next instant Helen heard the roar of her own blood. She'd given herself away; Julia hadn't said the man was married. She held her breath, bracing herself for the accusation that was sure to come. But miraculously, Julia didn't notice.

"I felt awful. But it didn't matter. I was hooked. I'd never have been able to end it myself."

"So he ended it?"

"No. Yes. In a sense." She took a deep breath and exhaled forcefully. "We had plans to meet for lunch. I went to the restaurant and waited. After a while I ordered. He was never late before, so I worried a little. My food came and I ate. I don't know why, but it was important to me to appear as though nothing was wrong. To look like a working woman eating alone on purpose. I waited to call until I got home. His assistant told me not to call again." She stopped to struggle with her voice. "I wrote a few times, and finally I got a letter from him, but it didn't really explain anything." She shrugged unhappily.

"You said he didn't love you . . ." Helen thought she couldn't hear that point repeated too often.

"Yes. I guess it was that simple, in the end."

"And then your husband left?"

"Pretty much."

"Wow."

Julia shrugged. "I know."

"You didn't think you should try to make your marriage work, for Peter's sake?"

Julia stood abruptly and visored her hand over her eyes as she watched the boys. Helen scrambled up, too, eager to hear her answer. In spite of herself, she'd begun

to find Julia's story compelling in its own right and had
to hear what happened next and next and next.

"Peter's all right," Julia said.

"Don't you think children need both parents,
though?"

Julia stiffened. "Children need a lot of things that
most of them don't get."

"But he *could* have had a normal family. If you'd kept
quiet . . ."

"If I'd stayed with my husband, Peter still wouldn't
be with his father."

It took Helen a few seconds to make sense of this; she
was so intent on aiming her own barb that at first she
accepted it coolly, as if it were just another bland sentence moving the conversation along. Then she got the
implication.

"Oh!" she gasped. "You mean—" She couldn't bring
herself to say it. She didn't know what to say. Her skin
crawled with horror. Never, not even on her worst
nights, had she imagined this.

"At least I still have something of him," Julia said.

"Oh," Helen said again and pressed her fingers to her
temples.

"I know. I made quite a mess, didn't I?"

What does she want from me, Helen wailed inwardly.
Does she really think I'm going to be sympathetic?
There was only one explanation for these sticky revela-
tions—that Julia was turning the tables on her and taking a revenge of her own. That must be it; how else

could she ram the knife of her confession into Helen's most vulnerable spot and then twist it so deftly?

Yet Julia had not shown any hint of excitement or tension or other telltale signs of scheming while delivering her bombshells. There was no discernible subtext beneath the emotions to which she openly laid claim. Either she was that rarity of rarities, Helen thought, a true female romantic—or else she was one great actress. It infuriated her that she wasn't sure which. In any case, she'd delivered an effective shock. If Peter was Nick's son . . . it was too awful to contemplate. Not only would Helen have to reassess what had happened in the past— if it was true, she'd kill Nick—but she'd also have to cope with the vast swath of possible repercussions, any of which might alter her future irrevocably. She recoiled even further as she remembered that one of her immediate reactions to the suggestion in Nick's card was a wave of empathy for Evan because of how a new child would affect his life. And that child would be *hers*.

"You *are* cold," Julia said.

Helen flinched—how had she betrayed herself? Then Julia pointed to the gooseflesh on her arms.

"It's getting chilly—it really feels like fall, doesn't it?"

Helen said nothing—though she was sure Julia could hear her heart smacking at her ribs.

"Anyway, Peter has an art class at five, so I must go. It's been nice chatting, though. Peter!" she called out.

At the sound of his mother's voice, the boy raised his

head. With a sick heart, Helen realized where she'd seen him before. He was the child she'd imagined when she was pregnant, Nick's child, with Nick's beauty, his elegance. He was her dream, a dream that had ended abruptly when Evan was born, forgotten until now. She felt a growing dread as the boys ran toward them.

"I don't want to go," Evan said. "I want to play with Peter."

"Maybe you two can get together again sometime," Julia said as she looked at him searchingly. Then she smiled at Helen. "Remember me to Nick, will you?"

Helen felt her jaw drop. She couldn't help it.

"It was nice to see you," Julia went on. "A nice surprise. As I said, I didn't think you liked me—I thought Nick disapproved. A touch of paranoia, I guess." She pulled Peter to her, mussed his silk hair.

"Nick disapproved?"

She nodded. "I confided in him, you see, about my friend. He didn't tell you? I always thought you had the kind of marriage where he told you everything."

Helen stared at her, dumbstruck.

"I told him about . . . my situation," Julia went on. "He wrote me a letter saying he didn't want to act in the role of confidant. I called and apologized, but I never heard from him again. I believe he thought I was a scarlet woman."

She blushed at her own characterization. Helen pointed to Peter. "You mean he isn't—"

Julia looked at her curiously.

"—Nick's son?" she whispered.

There was a pause, then Julia raised both hands to her mouth as her eyes lit up. "No, no. Oh my God. Is that what you thought?"

"I . . . well . . . look at him!" Helen spluttered.

Julia did as told, but apparently she couldn't see what was so clear to Helen. She turned back and shrugged.

"What?" she asked.

Helen wanted to shake her. Julia had started this, after all. "He looks just like—you know who."

"Really? I never thought of it. To me he looks exactly like—the other." She was quiet for a moment, then began to smile. "You thought there was something between me and Nick?"

Helen glanced at Evan, but he was too preoccupied with Peter to have noticed the mention of his father's name. She nodded at Julia.

"Oh dear! Oh, that's funny!" She seemed to play out the possibility in her mind; her expression grew more incredulous and amused as the scenes went by. Helen was dismayed to note she looked even lovelier as her spirits lightened.

"You've believed that all these years?" She was sympathetic, yet egregiously merry. "Poor Helen. I can assure you, you had nothing to worry about. What ever gave you the idea that—"

Julia broke off, leaving Helen to complete her question, as if it would be too creepy for her to even name the possibility. Helen bristled. She'd had her reasons, after all, for thinking what she thought. Even if she'd been wrong, she wasn't going to allow this woman to make her out to be ridiculous.

"I saw the letter, Julia."

"What letter?"

Helen raised her eyebrows. Who was being stupid now?

"The one he sent you? You mentioned it a moment ago."

"Oh."

"I saw it before he sent it." There. Let Julia cope with that bit of news.

"And didn't that clear things up? I mean, I remember that letter, and there was nothing romantic in it. I found it a little insulting, as a matter of fact."

"Insulting?" She wondered if they were talking about the same letter. Had Nick sent another that she didn't know about?

Julia nodded, displaying the victim's eagerness to complain about a slight. "I remember him saying something to the effect that he didn't agree with my morality, or his code prevented him from helping me. Something to that effect." She hugged herself, as if the blow was still fresh. "Wait—it's coming back to me. He used the word 'scruples.' I violated his scruples, apparently. It hurt me, to tell the truth. I threw it away immediately."

Scruples. Yes, he'd used that word. Helen thought of the line—*My own feelings—and scruples—prevent me from doing what you suggest.* For all these years, she was sure she'd known what he meant. The feelings he referred to were his feelings for her, Helen. The scruples were along the same lines, accessories to the feelings, bulwarks to guide the flow of his emotions. The way Julia had taken it—as a criticism of what she'd told him—was off the mark. But if Julia had been quick to believe he was talking about her, might not Helen have made the same mistake? What if there was yet a third meaning of that line, one that neither of them had considered? She thought of how he'd ended the letter: . . . *we cannot see each other anymore. I hope you'll understand.* Julia hadn't, but Helen was afraid she was beginning to. Perhaps the feelings Nick referred to were of a nature he didn't dare make clear. Perhaps . . . What if . . .

Immediately she saw them all at the restaurant again, saw Julia flirting; in her mind's eye Nick shifted uncomfortably and looked away. She'd thought he'd been bored, which thrilled her; she recalled putting that impression into words for him when they got home, and then, when she got no argument, going on to highlight everything Julia had said that betrayed the slightest hint of shallowness or stupidity, traits she knew he disliked. She remembered the surge of triumph she'd felt when he'd appeared to agree. But what if "appeared" was the operative word? What if he'd let her cut up Julia, had offered no defense of her whatsoever, because he didn't dare discuss her at all? Wouldn't that be exactly what a person would do if he wanted to hide his true feelings? What better subterfuge than a feigned distaste?

Helen began to pace, nearly oblivious to Julia and the children, as she continued to work the puzzle. Again she revisited the restaurant, this time watching from a slightly different vantage point. Suddenly it seemed that Julia was trying to draw *her* out while being no more than warm and friendly to Nick. Nick, meanwhile, was clearly in the grips of such a paralyzing attraction that he could barely look at Julia, or anybody; if he did, all would be revealed, so his answers came in dull monosyllables as he dug at his food. Finally Helen scanned around the table to Julia's husband, who appeared distracted and annoyed, but not by anything going on in his immediate surroundings. Yes, she decided, that was what had really happened. Moreover, it had been obvious. So how could she have been so obtuse?

She stopped in her tracks at the harshness of that word—she hated having to apply it to herself—but the plain fact of the matter was that she'd succumbed to the world's oldest temptation: she'd stubbornly believed what she wanted to believe, seeing everything by a light that favored her best angle. She'd wanted the feelings he'd referred to in the letter to be for her, so she'd assumed that was the case. That initial assumption had tainted every other thought on the subject. Now she saw that, actually, she'd only figured under the category of Nick's scruples, and there, probably only obliquely. The loyalty of which he'd spoken—written—was to the marriage, a fidelity that had more to do with ethics than romance. He'd be loyal no matter who he married. It was barely personal. In fact, it was entirely possible that when he wrote that letter to Julia, he wasn't thinking of Helen *at all*.

"You threw the letter away," she managed. This was a nightmare, the worst she'd ever had, awake or asleep. She thought she might scream or choke trying not to. "Well. Well, well, well."

"At least we got this straightened out!" Julia crowed. "It's crazy, isn't it, the things we do to ourselves?"

We. As if they were in this together. "Yes, it is crazy."

Julia neatened her appearance with a tug here, a smoothing there—all redundant efforts, thought Helen.

"On second thought, don't remember me to Nick. He really did hurt my feelings."

Helen felt herself lurch in defense of Nick. She couldn't stand Julia thinking him a jerk—that was *her* prerogative. "No he didn't," she said. "Or at least he didn't mean to."

"All right. Whatever." Julia's nostrils flared.

"Nick isn't a judgmental person, Julia. He wasn't criticizing you."

"It was a good imitation, then." Her lips grew tight, defensive. Helen saw Julia really had been hurt. What a mess! What a waste.

"His scruples weren't about you, Julia." Not everything is, she thought but didn't add. "He was talking about himself. He couldn't be your confidant because he couldn't bear to hear you talk about your feelings for someone else."

"I don't understand."

Helen wanted to get this over with, and the truth seemed the quickest way. What else was there now? "Julia. He couldn't fulfill the role you asked him to play in your life because he was in love with you himself."

Julia's jaw dropped. It was clear she'd had no idea. Helen recalled the miserable nights, the days of rage. Suddenly she had the odd thought that Nick, too, must have felt very lonely in those days, keeping such a secret. God help us all, she thought.

"Oh," Julia said. "Oh. That never crossed my mind. Oh, poor Nick." She shook her head, then looked up abruptly. "Poor you!"

Helen held up her hand to stave off the pity. "Anyway," she said. Enough was enough. She was weary to the bone and wondered how she'd make it through the evening. "We've got to go, too. Come say good-bye, Evan."

The boys dragged toward them again. Peter tugged on Julia's arm. "Can we go back to the rock?"

It was the uncanny symmetry of his features, Helen thought, that had reminded her of Nick; that was all. They didn't really resemble each other. Waves of hot shame rushed through her as she thought of what a fool she'd made of herself.

Julia sniffled. "No, no. Your lesson, remember?" She

167

turned to Helen. "I don't know what to say. I'm amazed." To Helen's surprise, she rubbed her nose on her sleeve. "It's nice to know there are good men left in the world. I wonder sometimes."

"Good?" Helen blurted. It was hardly the word she had for Nick at the moment. He'd betrayed her, even if he'd never let it show.

"Yes, good. Very good, really," Julia continued. "He cared enough not to tell either of us, which was the kindest thing he could have done. I wish I'd had his scruples. You're a lucky woman, Helen. And even if you didn't mean it before," Julia went on, "I think you're right, we could have been friends." She became a flurry of activity. "But it's not too late, is it? Look at how well these boys get along. We should get them together again, shouldn't we, and talk some more? Here's my number." She wrote, using her purse as a desk.

Out of reflex, Helen tucked the slip of paper into the pocket of her skirt. Then Julia ambushed her with a swift hug. "Good-bye, Helen, and thank you. It means a lot to know someone had real feelings for me. I appreciate your sharing it. I don't think I'd have been as generous." She took Peter's hand and began to walk away. "And happy birthday!" she called out without turning around.

Helen stared after her. Sharing! Generous! Lucky! What an idiot. Did she really think Helen might call? And then what—Helen would invite her over so she and Nick could become reacquainted? As if! The woman was living in a dream world. The first chance she had, Helen threw the slip of paper Julia had given her in a wastebasket.

"What was that, Mom?" Evan asked.

"Nothing," she told him.

Instantly she felt better, being rid of it—until she remembered she already knew Julia's number by heart.

Close

TASHA SOUNDED like a name out of a romance novel. Just this side of cloying. But great on her.

She was in his thoughts when Ian woke up. Immediately he buried his face in the pillow and moaned, but there was no relief in it. She'd been so close in this particular dream that he caught the exact scent of the skin between her nose and upper lip and, as if in slow motion, saw the muscles in her cheeks tighten as she looked up at him and smiled. He'd reached out to touch her and automatically snapped awake; that was how thoroughly he'd incorporated the precariousness of his situation. He couldn't even dream of her without feeling guilty, couldn't think of her without his stomach sloshing. The intensity of what he felt for her still surprised him; he didn't know where it came from or what to do about it. What he did know was that he had to do something, and soon. Tasha'd delivered an ultimatum. Choose, she pleaded, I can't take it anymore.

All right, he'd agreed. The truth was, he couldn't take it either. Ian was a married man, about to become a father, a responsible, reliable, thirty-one-year-old guy.

Not a kid anymore. And not the type to have an affair—
at least not until Tasha. He wasn't cut out for it, hated
the deceptions and the juggling; he believed in marriage, for God's sake. Although he had no idea how he'd
do it, he had to decide, and it had to be soon.

This weekend, he told himself. By Sunday night he'd
have an answer for Tasha. He would choose—but how?
He loved them both. He knew how crappy that
sounded, but it was true. Tasha had nothing to do with
his feelings for his wife, Margot. He wished she did;
then at least he'd have an excuse, albeit a shopworn one.
As it was, he had no explanation for his behavior except
that he was a jerk, a heel, a selfish bastard—epithets
that had ruined his sleep for weeks. He was definitely
ready to lead a clean life again. But with whom?

At least this weekend he'd have time to think without being swayed by seeing either of them. He was on a
business trip, in a businessman's motel, in a room with
two beds, a refrigerator, a microwave, a television en-
hanced by several premium channels, a hair dryer, a
phone (two, actually; there was also one in the bathroom)—*and* he'd brought along his laptop. "It's like an
apartment in Tokyo," he'd joked to Margot when
they'd spoken the night before. He could have gone
home already—he'd finished his meetings—but he'd
stayed on to have a look at the house where he'd lived as
a child. He hadn't seen it since he was twelve, when it
was sold during his parents' divorce. Tasha'd asked him
to take her there, which was impossible, of course—at

least for the moment. Margot also wanted to see it, had been suggesting it for years, but he'd always steered her toward less loaded destinations. Then this business trip came up. When he looked at the map, he saw he'd be only a few miles from the house.

"Oh, let's go," Margot had said. "Let's have one last fling before the baby comes. We'll take pictures, so we can show him later where you grew up."

He'd winced at the word "fling" and swiftly agreed to her suggestion. They'd made the plans, but in the end she'd decided it was getting too late in the pregnancy to travel that far from her doctor.

"Promise you'll take us again?" she said, meaning her and the baby, his coming-right-up son. Us was already *them*. It was tempting to resent that, to feel left out; in other words, to use it to justify Tasha. He fought the urge, though—he wasn't a complete sleaze.

"Of course," he agreed. "In fact, let's wait until we can all go together." He felt himself trying to buy time. He'd avoided that house and would be happy to go on doing so.

"No, no. You go. You can't miss this opportunity!" Margot shook her head, as if the very idea was madness. "I want a full report."

He sighed and sat up. A shard of sun was inching across the mauve rug, while a prism somewhere had tossed rainbows on the dark wood of the bedside table. Idly he dipped his hand into the pool of color and was transported immediately back to a fall day in his childhood dining room. He'd just come home from school and happened to walk in at the moment when the pine table was strewn with a display of spectral flags toward which he automatically reached. To his surprise, the flags had no substance. When he tried to grasp them, he ended up with an empty fist striped with colored light and a fretful wish that no one had seen him make such a fool of himself.

No such luck. His mother watched the whole episode from the kitchen door and the incident became a family story. Supposedly it demonstrated cuteness on his part, but he didn't feel cute. Even now, he found the anecdote humiliating and wondered that no one else recognized the pathos in the image of a boy who thought he could hold rainbows. For Ian the moment had become emblematic of his whole youth, which he thought of as a series of internal longings the pursuit of which either left him empty-handed or got him in trouble. Eventually he decided that the longings themselves must be off-base and had trained himself to live by a code of principles rather than according to his private emotions. Tasha was an exception that underscored the rule. He should break it off with her . . . but on the other hand, he thought, maybe it was time he tried again to listen to his inner voices. Maybe he was old enough to make his impulses work.

He glanced at the clock. It was only six, too early to disturb anyone. He couldn't call Tasha anyway, not until he had an answer for her, and he didn't want to

wake Margot. He realized the person he really wanted
to talk to was Bill, his father. Bill would listen without
judgment, but he'd have a clear idea of what Ian should
do. He wouldn't even mind being woken up to talk;
what were dads for? He lived alone in a breezy house in
Key West, which he'd bought dirt cheap in the seventies
after Ian's mother dumped him for being a loser—signi-
fied by his refusal to stop being a painter even when his
work didn't sell. His art did better in Florida, but he
drank a lot and had never exactly landed on his feet, at
least not in any northern sense. Nevertheless, Ian
thought him the wisest person he knew and felt lucky
to have him as a father. If anyone had the answer to this
problem, it would be Bill.

Ian dialed the number. No answer. He felt better for
trying, though, less alone. He tossed the covers back.

The fields were almost gone; it saddened him to see it.
He'd run himself sick in those fields, run until his lungs
felt scalded and his legs were so tight he feared the ten-
dons would snap. Now it was one development after the
next, expensive faux French houses sprouting incongru-
ously from the old Indian land. As a kid he'd found lots
of arrowheads buried in the dirt. He wondered if the
construction workers bothered to collect the artifacts
that they plowed up or if the children who lived in
these sterile houses ever went exploring. Did anyone
even think about what had been there once?

It wasn't all bad news, however. Though much of the

land had been ruined, the lay of it was the same, the streets still making for a bumpy ride that reminded him of pioneers being jostled on their buckboard wagons. With the windows down, the sharp clean scents of forsythia and thawing ground lent his flimsy rental car the purity of his old Raleigh three-speed, and he found himself instinctively shifting his weight as he maneuvered along the twisting roads that were known for disorienting even the locals. This is good, he thought— good to remember who he was before women. The radio featured an album side of early Springsteen, and that seemed right, too.

He took the "back way" to Mill Rock Road and felt a pang as he turned the final corner and entered the street. The shade trees had grown, but the curbs were still buried under the detritus of leaves and mock oranges and black walnuts, a natural arsenal perfect for chucking at cars. He noticed the Millers had a red door now and an addition had been built onto the side of Drew Adams's, except they weren't the Millers' or the Adamses' houses anymore; all the mailboxes declared new names. At the front of every property, large leaf bags sat lined up for collection by the township in compliance with the spate of laws against leaf burning that had overtaken the suburbs since he was a kid. That was too bad, he thought. He'd loved looking out his window at night and seeing a circle of embers shining in the back yard, then lying down on sheets that smelled of cooked leaves. In the afternoons, he'd send the buoyant ashes flying with a stamp of his foot and write his name surreptitiously on the blind side of the garage with the tip of a charred stick. What did kids do now, he wondered. What was childhood without campfires? Somehow or other, he thought, he'd give his own son that experience.

He swallowed repeatedly as he approached the end of the cul-de-sac, site of his family's house. The night before he'd fantasized about ringing the doorbell and asking to have a look around. He'd even lingered over an image of himself pointing out to the current children the spot in the attic where he'd carved his name in the rafters. What he hadn't imagined was what he saw now—a carefully lettered green-and-white For Sale sign planted in the middle of the front yard. It threw him for a moment; was it really possible that someone other than his heartless mother was capable of abandoning this house? He realized he still held to the notion that she was singularly insensitive. Now *that* was an insight for Margot, he thought; she was always encouraging him to do some therapy. Maybe she was right, he told himself quickly, not wanting to feel snippy toward her. His chest ached, though, from missing Tasha.

A face appeared at one of the upstairs windows. He gave a reassuring wave and pointed to the realtor's sign, meaning to suggest he'd return under official auspices, that he wasn't some creep casing the joint. As he drove off it occurred to him that it was actually a stroke of luck that the house was for sale. He could take a look without making a big deal of it. Tasha would want him to go for it, to make the most of the opportunity; Margot would be thrilled if he brought her the realtor's write-up so she'd have a picture, details, stats. Of course, depending on what he decided about the future, he might not have the chance to tell one or the other of them much about this part of his trip. But that was a concern for later, when he'd made a decision. At the moment, he knew that they each would like him to take a tour. It seemed the least he could do.

"May I use the phone?" he asked. "I have a calling card."

The receptionist smiled and wheeled her chair to the far end of her desk to give him privacy. It was a moot point, however; his father still didn't answer. Ian shrugged and handed the receiver back.

"Anything important?" the receptionist asked sympathetically.

"It can wait," Ian said. In this context, importance surely denoted a business problem. Yet the woman behind the desk seemed to hint at a willingness to be a sounding board. Ian felt a wad of emotion rise behind his ribs as he contemplated what a relief it would be to spill his guts. Why not confide in her? It would be like talking to a stranger in a bar, harmless and comforting. He tapped his fingers on the desk and opened his mouth to speak. "Uh," he began, then felt a knot the size of a squash ball settle at the base of his throat. He drummed his fingers more rapidly, shrugged again, and walked back to the sofa where he'd originally been told to wait. There was a listings book on a coffee table and he was beginning to thumb through it when Tommy Wood came rushing through the door. His good leather shoes grated on the tile, a sound that Ian associated with work, focus, success. Good for Tommy, he thought—or Tom now, surely. The receptionist spoke to him, leaning eagerly forward, and pointed over at Ian. Tom turned toward him wearing his professional mask, then broke into a grin.

"Ian Flynn. What do you know." Tom's handshake was dry and warm.

"More than I did the last time you saw me, I hope," Ian laughed. They'd been classmates.

Tom didn't take this as a joke. "That's good," he said solemnly. He hadn't let go yet, and now brought his other hand up, pressing Ian's into a sandwich. "Not everyone can claim that."

Ian blushed, feeling he'd misrepresented himself. "Well, I don't know if I can, either," he backpedaled.

Tom gazed at him with a ministerial benevolence. It was a look Ian recognized but rarely encountered in New York, Dale Carnegie redux. He had to stifle an impulse to laugh, and the laughter caught in his chest like a pill swallowed dry. Tom led Ian to his office and showed him to a chair that afforded a view of what appeared to be the only raw field left along the commercial strip. A pretty woman in a burgundy pantsuit came in and handed them each a fragrant cup of coffee. She called Tom "Mr. Wood," but said it in an exaggerated, almost facetious way that made the hair rise on Ian's arms. He tried to appear preoccupied as they exchanged glances, but he registered every nuance. As she left, Ian automatically craned toward the picture of Tom's wife and kids on the desk.

"I married Kay Nelson," Tom said, following Ian's gaze. "Do you remember her?"

"Sure. She looks great." Ian inspected the photograph more thoroughly, but he couldn't separate her out from the river of girls who'd been at the junior high, all of whom had astonished him. In the picture, Kay Nelson Wood—he doubted women kept their names around here—looked like Pam Dawber from *Mork & Mindy*, a pretty brunette. He wondered if she suspected anything.

"We have twin girls, Ruthie and Miranda. Do you have a family?" Tom asked.

Ian still thought of his parents and sibs as his family. He wondered if that would change when his kid was born. "My wife is pregnant."

To Ian's surprise, Tom made a revolted frown that did away with the Dale Carnegie demeanor. "That's a drag. I mean, it's great about the baby, but jeez. Let's just say that was not my favorite moment, and it lasted thirty-eight weeks. Maybe you're into it, though. Some guys really are."

Ian had a sudden memory of Tommy clutching his

stomach and rolling on the ground in a pastiche of pain after someone had appeared in the locker room brandishing a used tampon in a plastic bag. Ian had envied his show of squeamishness; his sisters had bullied that out of him and enjoined him to be respectful and mature about everything to do with girls' bodies. Now he felt a bubble of mirth in his gut at the prospect of admitting his own discombobulation, for the truth was he couldn't get used to the way Margot looked pregnant. She'd always had pretty limbs which, if anything, had been improved by the layer of extra fat plumping her skin. She was as ripe and glowing as a polished apple; he could feel himself blush Harrison Fordishly when he looked at her. Most remarkably, her former moodiness was miraculously gone, osmosed into the hormone bath that had swept her off to a tranquil, dreamy place from which she gazed out at him as if he were far, far away. He couldn't get used to it. He leaned forward.

"You know what happened once?" Ian said. "I was walking on Fifth Avenue and I saw a woman waving at me from across the street. I cringed for her, waving like that to a stranger. Then I realized she was my wife!"

Tommy nodded. "Yeah, it's weird. And those sonograms! Kay kept looking at the tape, oohing and aahing. I finally asked her how she knew those were our kids. Who's to say they don't show the same tape to everybody?"

"Good point," Ian said. "I never thought of that."

"Kay told me that wasn't funny."

"I'm sure. Margot has no sense of humor about it, either. And every time she has a doctor appointment, she
goes into one of the baby shops on Madison Avenue and
buys a new outfit. We're going broke dressing someone
who doesn't even exist yet!"

Tom leaned back in his chair and fiddled with a pen.
"And guess what? It only gets worse. Your marriage is
basically over, pal. From now on, you're a meal ticket.
You'll walk into the house at night and you'll feel like
a stranger. Remember that Talking Heads song where
he says, 'This is not my beautiful house, this is not
my beautiful wife'? Pretty soon that will *start* making
sense!"

Ian got the reference and acknowledged it with the
sort of grimace one makes at a pun. Part of him cringed
at being drawn into a conversation that was clearly
heading in the direction of disloyalty, but another part
clamored with relief at the prospect of confession. He
hadn't told anybody about his situation. Bill was going
to be the first, whenever Ian was finally able to reach
him. Yet perhaps it would be better to get advice from
someone his own age? He didn't know Tommy, but then
again he did; he knew him in the way that one knows
childhood friends, a visceral knowing that included
habits and proclivities that had since been quashed. He
and Tommy knew each other's families, how their
houses had smelled, what they ate, and how they
treated each other. That had validity, Ian thought.
There were truths there that outweighed much of what

had happened since. And chances were, he wouldn't see Tommy again anyway; there was no crossover between their lives. He decided to take the risk.

"So what would you do if you met somebody else?"

Tommy laughed. "I've met a lot of other people."

"Someone special, I mean."

There was a pause. Tommy tapped his pen against his palm and glanced at the door through which the woman in the burgundy pantsuit had disappeared. Ian breathed lightly, from the top of his chest. His pulse roared.

"I'd be careful," Tom said without looking up.

"Yeah." Ian felt queasy. He wasn't sure if Tommy was making a confession or offering a warning.

"You have to consider the kids." Now Tommy raised his eyes. "Right?"

Ian nodded. His parents had gotten the first divorce among their crowd, although many others weren't far behind, Tommy's parents included. "Right," he muttered. He wondered briefly if he could convince Tasha to go on as they were, but the thought fluttered from his mind like a leaf, dead and spiraling. It was useless.

Tommy smiled, a salesman again. "So you heard your parents' old house was for sale. Are you really interested, or do you just want to take a look?"

"B," Ian said.

"Hey, why not? You know who lives there, don't you? Wallace Muldoon. Speaking of divorce!"

"You're kidding. Wallace lives there now?"

Ian reached for the phone. "Not for much longer, I guess. I know he'd get a kick out of seeing you. Why don't you have some more coffee while I try to reach him? I'm pretty busy today, but you could go over without me, couldn't you? And if you decide you want to make a bid, you'll call me back."

Before Ian could protest—he usually limited himself to a cup a day—the woman in the burgundy pantsuit appeared and poured refills for them both.

Had snow been in the forecast? Ian hadn't paid attention. All he knew was that while he was in Tom's office the sky whitened, and as he reached his car the windshield was budding fat, wet flakes.

He'd loved Christmas in the Mill Rock Road house. His parents knew how to celebrate, that was for sure. His mother wound strands of ribbon and pine around the bannister and sprayed powdered snow stencils onto the windows. Bill made a big deal out of getting the tree. They sold them at the firehouse, where the volunteer firemen created a festive atmosphere by dressing up in bits and pieces of Santa costumes and roasting chestnuts and marshmallows over old oil barrels filled with fragrant logs.

Everyone knew everyone else, and the kids hurled snowballs and played hide and seek among the merchandise while the parents exchanged last-minute invitations and details of holiday plans. Eventually choices were made and the great, shivering trees were tied to the tops of station wagons for the ride home. See you at church, people called out of frosty windows. See you later at the Flynns'! Trails of warm breath rose like breakaway balloons through the crisp air as dozens of hands—mittens, gloves—waved merry good-byes. All around the neighborhood lights were draped over bushes and wound around fence posts; at night, the separate plots converged into a single entity and it was impossible to tell where one property ended and the next began. It was all for one and one for all, a charming, glittery place in the universe where the meaning of life was clear, children were safe, and families stayed together.

Ian sighed. He wished he could make himself believe that he'd actually be doing his son a favor by leaving now rather than possibly later, but he knew that was just wishful b.s. He sifted through Tommy's statements again and decided that, taking all factors into consideration, his advice had been to stay with Margot. All right, all right, Ian thought, nodding—who could argue with that? But the comeback was swift and obvious; Tom didn't know Tasha. Ian wasn't sure he could stand to never spend a Christmas with her.

Wallace answered the door and grabbed Ian into a bear hug. Although Ian couldn't have predicted what he'd grow up to look like, he saw Wallace as basically the same, small-eyed and chinless. Now he was heavy and balding but his childhood face shone through. He still looked like trouble for the teacher.

"This is perfect," Wallace bellowed. "Everyone's out. You want a beer?"

Ian pointed to the window. "It's getting slippery out there. I'd better not."

Wallace opened the fridge. "I'm not going anywhere. At least not today." He popped the tab on the can and ran to the sink, cupping the escaping froth. "Not that it matters what I do anymore. Here's to marriage," he toasted sarcastically. "Are you married?"

Ian nodded. "And expecting."

"Then I'll try to spare you my current vitriol." He swigged hard. "Although I can't claim I didn't bring this on myself."

"How?" Ian asked.

"You don't want to know."

"Yeah, I do." Wallowing with Wallace. Why not?

Wallace caught the hint in his tone and squinted more ferociously. "Okay, but let me give you the tour first. All the rooms are pretty much the same . . ."

They were. It was weird. As Ian walked through the house, he was easily able to remember everything, and none of it hurt as much as he'd expected. His initials were still on the rafter and that gave him a buzz, but otherwise, to his chagrin, it was just a house. Once, during college, he'd been in a car that drove nearby, and he'd purposely slept until they were clear of the area. He couldn't stand the idea of seeing it occupied by other people. It was his, his touchstone, the haven of stability and comfort that had formed a needed counterbalance to his parents' troubles. Or so he'd thought. Now he felt an idiot for having made so much of it over the years. Luckily Wallace kept up a constant patter as they moved about so Ian didn't have to say much. He confined his comments to murmurs of appreciation when Wallace indicated pride in a particular corner or room. Ian's old room, for instance, now contained a loft bed with a desk underneath it that Wallace had built himself for his son.

"It has to stay here," Wallace said regretfully. "I can't take it apart. I didn't think I'd have to."

Ian gave his arm a steadying squeeze. "So what happened?" He'd seen enough and was ready to talk.

Wallace shrugged. "I met someone."

Ian knew that, it had been clear from their exchange in the kitchen, but it was still exciting to hear it stated, and so casually.

"Oh."

"Oh is right. Come on, let's go into the den. In case they come back."

They clambered downstairs and into what used to be, in Ian's day, a combination play/ironing/guest room, the decor muddled and in flux. It occurred to him now that it was the room that reflected the true state of his family, as opposed to the show of propriety put forth by the dining room or the pretension of the living room. He closed his eyes for a moment and remembered it; how clear it had been for anyone willing to look at the clues that his mother had been on her way out the door for a long time before she finally left. There'd been travel brochures and fashion magazines in piles along the wainscoting, all wizened from handling. He wondered what nook of the apartment showed his state of mind but he couldn't place anything in particular. He thought he was too close to see himself clearly; he was in it too deep.

"I'm going to miss this room," Wallace said.

Ian cast a glance around. The space was a pastiche of masculinity, complete with a Foosball table and a mounted collection of beer coasters. It depressed him, but he welcomed that sensation. It fit with the snow and his worries. Wallace pointed him to a beat-up old leather armchair; he couldn't remember when he'd felt as physically comfortable. To complete the picture, Wallace lit up a cigar.

"You mind if I take a nap?" Ian joked.

"It's good, eh? I call it my home away from home at home. I'll be sorry to leave this, too."

"So—are you going to be with your friend?" Ian was amazed his voice didn't crack like a kid's.

"Funny you should ask that. That's the million-dollar question in my mind. What happened was, my wife found out and raised hell and made appointments with shrinks and all this crap, so I broke it off with Susan. I bought into the whole thing of owing the marriage a second chance; that sounded reasonable. I mean, we've got three kids. Then my wife says she just can't get over it and never will and wants a divorce. So I call Susan but she says it's too late—how could she ever trust me again?"

"Wow."

"I know. I mean it would be funny if it weren't so fucking frustrating."

Ian shuddered. It wasn't funny. He could picture the scenario all too well. "So what are you going to do?"

"Well, we have to sell this place. She's going to get a smaller house and I'm moving to an apartment in Philadelphia. I want to get a loft, you know? I'd have room for when the kids come over, and for some partying, too."

"Isn't it hard to live here now?"

Wallace gave a gruesome laugh. "It's sick is what it is. It doesn't help with Susan, either. But all our money— of which there isn't any, anyway—it's all frozen. I can't move out. I can't do anything. They say marriage is a trap, but it's nothing compared to this!"

Ian nodded. What could he say?

"The worst part is, I have no one to blame but myself. I wanted to be with Susan, but I was too fucking chicken to do it when I had the chance. Now it's looking like I never will."

Suddenly Ian felt like laughing. The conversation was absurdly apropos. Who am I, he thought, Ebenezer Scrooge, being haunted? The reference brought him back to images of Christmas, and again he felt the tears rise. Wallace switched the subject to Ian, but Ian focused on work and anecdotes rather than telling his story. He didn't know how it ended yet.

That night he woke up with a swollen heart. It was only one o'clock but he dressed and went out to the lobby to stave off the stabbing thoughts that were liable to come in the dark. No one else was up, and the building was swathed in the quiet that fell after snow. Ian walked to the shelf of books in the front parlor. A handwritten index card—an attempt at calligraphy—instructed guests to take or leave the volumes as they wished. His eyes lit on a collection of Fitzgerald; perfect. He reached for it greedily, looking forward to having his own mood of regret and longing put into words. "Winter Dreams," he thought, or maybe even "Babylon Revisited," which always made his throat constrict. This was good—a familiar route to help him toward an unknown destination. He didn't kid himself that there weren't other people who knew how he was feeling, but F. Scott could put it into words.

After settling himself, however, on a rather scratchy sofa, he began to probe the image on the dust jacket; he realized it was the same edition his father had kept on his bedside table when Ian was a small boy. The lamp nearby cast a comfortable light on the text, but the words of even his favorite stories blurred under the pressure of his driving thoughts. It was not the first time that he'd felt so alone, but always before he'd assumed the extremity of the feeling was temporary. Now he felt utterly desolate, hopeless. His former methods of staying tough and impenetrable seemed to have forsaken him; as if wanting to get away from himself, he sprang off the sofa and began to pace.

Absentmindedly he wove a path in and out of the furniture until he ended up by the pay phone in the foyer. Of course; he'd been headed toward a telephone all along. As he lifted the receiver, it occurred to him that in spite of her instructions not to call until he'd made a choice, on some level Tasha was waiting for him to call, and that she would see it as a strength rather than a weakness when he finally did. He thought of her face as it looked in an attitude of pleasure and how thoroughly it moved him to be a source of happiness for her. She made him feel ten feet tall. Even in his current anguish the memory of her voice stood out from his own internal chatter, and he heard again her remonstrations.

"You'll be alive and I'll be alive but we won't be married to each other?"

She was right; it was nuts. He knew the shape of her telephone number by heart and pressed it without looking at the buttons, thereby feeling a sense of dominion over the mechanics of the situation that translated, for a heady moment, into a belief that he was doing the right thing. But when the telephone began to ring . . . he couldn't call Tasha. Hadn't his sisters taught him years earlier to assume that no meant no? As he replaced the receiver in its cradle he thought he heard her voice, and her hopeful tone filled him with a remorse that literally doubled him over. When he could breathe again, he walked outside.

The moon lit the frosted cars in the parking lot as efficiently as a series of lamps. He crossed the street and followed the path by the riverbank. The snow had mostly melted, although there was still some in strips along the branches and held in clumps of downed leaves. Out of a childhood habit, he skidded down the bank to examine a beaver dam and was gratified to see it studded with the same brands of candy wrappers he remembered from twenty years earlier. The bits of foil and aluminum bottle caps that littered the silt bottom shone a precious light up toward the sky. He and Tasha had often spoken about how deeply they appreciated the natural world, and he'd said she was all of nature to him. It was true; no matter how hard he fought it, she was present in these lacy branches, this spongy earth. She was a part of his life, a presence. If that made him a terrible person, he'd have to live with it.

He went back to the lobby and pressed Bill's number.

"Dad?"

"Ian! I just walked in. What are you doing up? I thought you kept bankers' hours."

"I have to ask your advice."

"Shoot, son."

"I will. But first—guess where I went today. Mill Rock Road."

"Do I need a beer to hear about this? I think so. Hold

on a minute." There was a pause, then all the noises of a flip top being ripped away. "Okay. Here I am. So how was the place?"

"Chilly."

"Those old houses are always chilly at this time of year. The damp seeps right through the walls."

"I saw my initials still carved in the attic."

"How about the trees? How big is the lilac now?"

"I didn't notice."

"I planted that for your mother on the anniversary of our first full year in the house. In those days, it was all she asked for, if you can believe it!"

Ian felt a rush of embarrassment, as if he were responsible for his mother's descent into materialism. "I'm sorry, Dad."

"How is she, anyway?"

"Fine. As always."

"Looking forward to her next grandchild?"

"I think so. She says she is."

Bill sighed. "She loves babies. Count yourself lucky. I'm sure she'll come over whenever you want, to baby-sit so you and Margot can get some time alone to remember why you liked each other. We didn't have that. Our families lived too far away."

"Is that what happened? You forgot how you felt in the beginning?" Ian felt himself grasping and angling toward his confession, his plea for help.

"Oh, I don't know. It was a long time ago, son."

"But you must still think about it."

"Not if I can help it."

"Really?"

"Really. As a matter of fact, let's change the subject right now. Tell me about the house," he said.

"Wait, Dad—" Ian was trying to figure out a way to launch into his Tasha story when he had a sudden image of Margot wearing his sweatshirt. When he'd spoken to her earlier, she said it was hard for her to sleep without him; maybe she was awake now? Maybe he should get in the car and go home early to surprise her. Before Tasha, he would have done that.

"Ian? Are you there?"

"I'm here, Dad."

"It must have been hard, eh? I mean, I couldn't go back there. Not if you paid me."

"Yes, you could," Ian said automatically. Then he winced and wished he could take it back. Who was he to say what Bill could or could not handle? Bill had bought that house. It had been his life, his marriage that went wrong there. Ian cleared his throat. "And someone *is* paying me," he said, hoping he sounded light. "I'm on a beeswax trip. The trip to the house was a tax deduction."

They laughed. "Okay," Bill went along with the joke. "Maybe if I got paid enough." There was a pause. "So what did you want to ask me?"

"Never mind. I think I figured it out."

"Are you sure?"

"No!" Ian laughed. "But I will be. I think it's some-thing I have to deal with on my own."

"Fine. So back to the house . . ."

Ian wound the phone cord around his finger. "Dad? I'm kind of tired. Can I call you tomorrow?"

"I'm not going anywhere."

"I'll call you."

Back in his room, Ian got into bed and pulled the cov-ers up. It was so dark he saw nothing even with his eyes wide open.

"I need a sign," he said aloud, but it didn't work any magic. The room was still and silent, absent of even the whisper of a passing car.

Maniacs

SILENT SOUND, vivid absence, pressure from beyond the quilts and walls, the taste of pennies on the tongue; several miles apart two sisters awoke within moments of each other and instinctively knew it had snowed. Diana, the little sister at thirty-four and still known as the pretty one, didn't even have to confirm it by looking; she smiled; hadn't she prayed for this? She had, all week, and her prayers had worked! The children wouldn't have to go now, not today at least.

Thick mugs of melted chocolate, a fierce, popping fire, Scrabble, a pillowy camp in the living room—Margaret had the same picture in mind as she hurried to the window and snapped the curtains open, her toes curling away from the bitter floor. She was the type of slender, well-proportioned blonde who made a good figure and platinum hair seem prim and unassailable rather than desirable and obvious. She was capable of feeling a secret wildness, though, and the thought of the storm that had come through overnight stirred her. She leaned her forehead against the cold glass and looked out.

It was still snowing, albeit gently now, just the final

fat, ineffectual flakes. A fresh coat of white covered the frozen crust that had covered the ground in Wynnemoor for weeks, and the lower branches of the old pine were buried except for a smattering of green-black fronds that emerged yards from the tree, looking freakish and disconnected.

There was a girlish second when Margaret swayed a little, imitating the drifts on the windward side of the house, but she couldn't allow herself to think of the potential pleasures for long; the skies were calming; the children would go. She dialed the airline and pulled her navy-blue christening-wedding-funeral suit out of the closet. If there was any problem about the girls' reservations or seats, Margaret believed she could prevail more easily if she were respectably dressed. Duncan Abbott, her ex-husband, had always compared her to Princess Anne when she wore this particular item. Good riddance to him, she thought as she lay the suit on the chaise and picked bits of lint off the pleats. At least now she could enjoy her clothes.

She'd just run a bath when the telephone rang. Probably Duncan, she thought; she wouldn't put it past him to be up at four in the morning, calling with a last-minute request for the girls to have some obscure piece of equipment with them when they arrived. In the past couple of weeks she'd bought snorkels, in-line skates, rubber swimming shoes. She wished she could trust him to purchase safe equipment, but as always, if she wanted it done right, she had to do it herself. She certainly couldn't get out to a store this morning, though. She'd have to send it express, whatever it was.

She grabbed the receiver, irritated, hoping the ring hadn't woken the girls. She wanted to let them sleep as late as was practical; she doubted they'd have a bedtime at Duncan's.

"What now?" she asked, without even saying hello.

It wasn't Duncan, though.

"Hurrah, hurrah," Diana cheered. "Let it snow! Now the girls can stay home."

Margaret wondered at Diana's perpetual wishful thinking. "No, they can't. Their plane is three hours late, that's all. They're going."

"You're not going to let them fly in this weather!"

"Why not?" Margaret crossed to her dressing table and picked up a nail file. She had a whole list of ways to use the time she spent on the telephone.

"It's dangerous. Think of all the planes that have crashed because of icing. You're giving a lot of credit to the greedy people who make these decisions."

"Oh, Diana." Margaret looked at the trees, the glassed branches, and hoped the gardener would remember his promise—she'd made him promise before signing a contract with him—to always plow her driveway first.

The girls were flying to visit their father at his new place in California, their first extended stay with him since the divorce. The night before, as she read in the living room, Margaret heard sounds she thought were

squirrels in the walls; but as she approached the stair-
case, she realized it was the girls, tiptoeing back and
forth to each other's rooms, whispering. Go to sleep,
she called out, and the footsteps stopped. Later she'd
wanted to look in on them, watch them sleep, but they'd
reached the age when they'd taken to shutting their
doors. "Anyway, I couldn't postpone the trip if I wanted
to. There's a legal agreement, remember."

"Laws are made to be broken."

"Not this one. I can't afford another court battle."

Diana gave an exasperated sigh. "All right. I give up
for now. Maybe you'll change your mind when we get to
the airport and you see the condition of the planes."

"When *we* get to the airport?"

"I'm going with you," Diana said. "I promised the
girls I would."

"When did all this happen?"

"Yesterday. When I was helping them pack. They're
nervous about seeing Duncan, Marg."

"You should have asked me first."

There was a pause. Margaret heard a match strike.

"You'll be glad I came when the car gets stuck in the
snow and I'm there to help shovel," Diana said.

Margaret considered whether or not it was worth arguing about this. She had to pick her battles with Diana
the same as she did with the children. Little did Diana
know how much she'd helped prepare Margaret for
motherhood.

"All right. We'll pick you up at eleven. Be outside, please, and *please* don't repeat your paranoid plane crash fantasies to the children."

"I'm not an idiot."

"No comment."

"See you," Diana singsonged and hung up.

In the bathroom, Margaret hung her nightdress behind the door and plunged swiftly into the water. The bottom of the old cast-iron tub was cold against her back. She picked up her loofah and went to work, scuffing her pale skin and coaxing the blood to the surface. Scrub, scrub, scrub, until she ached. Of course the children were nervous about seeing Duncan. He'd made Margaret nervous for fifteen years. Diana always thought she was so insightful, especially when it came to the girls. Margaret wished Diana would hurry up and get married and have children of her own, so she wouldn't be so obsessed with Allie and Evie. She'd drifted for long enough. She was probably back in bed right now, sleeping the morning away. Never mind, never mind, Margaret told herself. She had enough to worry about. In just a few hours, the girls would be gone.

"Looks like we have some time to kill. Shall we play I Spy?" Diana asked as they got into the long check-in line.

The girls glanced at each other in mute consultation. They were only a year apart but they looked nothing alike; Allegra was narrow and dusky while Evangeline was freckled and fair. But they were very close, like an old married couple, and alternated between bickering and putting up a united front against the rest of the world. At eleven and twelve, they'd reached the stage when people such as the man in the booth at the parking garage addressed them as "young ladies," and they were consequently wary of backsliding into the leagues of mere children. Margaret half expected them to reject Diana's suggestion, but Allie cocked her head and nodded, signaling that this situation was an exception to whatever their current rules might be.

"All right," Evie said, announcing their silent consensus.

"Good!" Then Margaret headed off a predictable squabble between the girls by insisting she go first. "I spy something blue."

Diana rolled her eyes.

"Not interesting enough for you?" Margaret challenged.

Diana raised her hands in a defensive gesture. "I didn't say anything."

"You don't have to."

"No fighting, no biting," Evie said.

"We're not fighting," Margaret and Diana said simultaneously. Diana laughed. "One-two-three-four-five-six-seven-eight-nine-ten you owe me a Coke," she said.

"What does that mean?" Evie asked. Margaret always marveled at Evie's femininity. She was the kind of girl

Margaret always envied when she was little, the kind afraid of spiders and disturbed by dead birds and mud. Margaret hadn't been, and when she'd tried to fake that range of sensitivity, she thought she came across as a jerk. She couldn't believe she'd produced a daughter who could shriek with the best of them.

"It's what we used to do after we said something at the same time," Diana explained. "Except both people are supposed to participate in the race. Margaret is a party pooper."

Diana wrinkled her lip at the girls, who took the cue and giggled at Margaret's expense. Great, Margaret thought. It hadn't taken long for Diana to get on her nerves. During the drive to the airport she'd prattled on ad nauseam about a man she'd met at a party the weekend before. As usual, her fantasies were way ahead of reality, to the point where she engaged the girls in a silly, in-depth discussion about possible bridesmaid dresses. Evie wanted gingham and a big bonnet, and Allie said she'd seen a fashion spread on black bridesmaid dresses in a magazine and thought they looked cool.

"Your mother would never wear a black matron-of-honor dress," Diana said. "Would you, Marg?"

"Not even in hell," she'd answered.

She hadn't meant to be funny, but the girls roared. She laughed, too, in an involuntary burble that caused a pain in her chest. Finally she brought the conversation back down to earth by asking Diana a few practical questions about this prince, such as what he did for a living, what his last name was, and why wasn't he married at his age. Diana didn't know the answer to any of them.

"He was nice," Diana said. "And cute," she added, winking at the girls. "What more is there?"

An hour later, Margaret was still annoyed by that exchange. She wished Diana wouldn't fill the girls' heads with romantic garbage. Especially not when they were about to spend time with their father, about whom she wanted them to have some perspective.

"I spy something blue," Margaret repeated. "Any guesses?" She pushed the girls' suitcase—her big old suitcase—forward with her foot. Kicked it, really.

"Is it that man's scarf?" Evie asked, pointing at someone a few check-in lines away.

They all turned to look. Margaret wasn't sure of the order in which things happened next—whether she spotted Jerome Strauss before Diana gasped or vice versa. Either way, there he was.

For a long time—too long—Margaret had looked for Jerome wherever she went. She had no right to, he'd never been her boyfriend; he'd liked Diana from the moment they met him at a proper old hotel in Florida where he was on spring vacation with his parents as they were with theirs. Diana had seen him on and off for years. Everyone assumed they'd get engaged sometime after college, but their relationship continued much as before, on-again, off-again, and befuddling to all observers. When you asked Diana about Jerome, you were as liable to hear that she was over him and seeing someone else as you were to hear his news. He disappeared from her conversation for months at a time; then, suddenly, Diana would be obsessing over him again, in her own utterly self-referential way.

"What do you think he's going to give me for Christmas?" she'd ask. Or, "He's going to love me in this dress."

Margaret inured herself to Diana's patter as best she could. It was difficult not to blurt out the truth, though, difficult not to shout out loud that she was the one who really loved Jerome, deeply, constantly, and so truly that she had the strength to keep it to herself. She continued to love Jerome for years, even after he and Diana broke up for good and he moved to Texas, which—to her—was the equivalent of disappearing from the face of the earth. It wasn't until somewhere between the births of her two daughters that Margaret had stopped looking for him, stopped imagining she'd spotted the back of his head, that it was him a few rows away in the movie theater or that he was the man who had just rounded the corner and slipped out of sight.

She didn't forget him, however. After Duncan moved out she reread her old diaries, searching for the passages about Jerome. They were even more intense than she remembered; she was tempted to make copies of a few particularly avid excerpts for Duncan, who'd accused her of lacking passion. She didn't do it, though—her feelings for Jerome were none of Duncan's business.

After her reading had buoyed her she'd put the diaries back in the attic. They were like money tucked in a mattress, insurance for bad times. For a while, in her shock and loneliness, she obsessed over the memory of Jerome, but even at her lowest, she never actually believed she'd ever see him again.

Now, here he was, standing just a few airline check-in counters away. She found herself alternately straining to get a better view and foolishly glancing around at her fellow travelers—she didn't want to look at Diana—to see if anyone else was showing signs of the amazement she felt, as if he were universally recognizable. She noted the ironic flair with which he reached into the inside pocket of his jacket for his ticket, making fun of big shot types. The woman behind the counter began her work perfunctorily, but was soon leaning forward, offering him private smiles that she no doubt ordinarily withheld; so, Margaret thought wryly, he hasn't lost his touch.

Instinctively, she looked up at the overhead monitor and wondered which flight he would be taking. She didn't see any flights to Texas listed; perhaps he was making a connection somewhere, like Atlanta, or St. Louis, or . . . Margaret stopped herself. In the present case, such calculation was particularly pointless, as there was no chance that she might be on his flight, no chance of it at all. The children were flying to California. Margaret wasn't going anywhere.

"Do you see what I see?" Diana said in a low voice, as if he might somehow hear her.

"I do," Margaret said.

"He hasn't changed." Diana continued to stare. "He's exactly the same. Even his hair."

Jerome's hair was the clear shimmery gray-brown of a pond in the fall. He wore it loose and long. He looked like Jesus.

"Who are you talking about?" Allie asked.

"An old friend of Diana's is here," Margaret said.

"Oh. An old boyfriend," Allie said knowingly.

Diana gave a pained smile and laid her hand on Allie's shoulder.

"Am I the only one playing this game?" Evie asked.

"I'm sorry. Take a guess."

"I just did. Is it that woman's shoes?"

Margaret said that was indeed what she'd had in mind. She'd actually been thinking of the navy uniforms on the airline personnel, but what difference did it make? Diana was right: blue was everywhere. "So it's your turn."

"Let me think for a minute," Evie said self-consciously.

"I can't believe it's really him," Diana said, mostly to herself. Neither can I, Margaret thought, feeling the same queasy lift in her stomach that used to overcome her whenever she thought of him. It was easy to hide her own emotion; she'd always done so. Diana had never had any idea how Margaret really felt.

"Which one is he? I want to see," Allie said.

Diana pointed. The girls raised up on their toes.

"You liked him? He looks like a hippie." Allie fixed Diana with a gaze that combined curiosity with disapproval. In her consternation, Margaret was sorry to note, Allie resembled Duncan Abbott.

"I think he looks nice," Evie said. "And looks aren't everything anyway. How old were you when you knew him?"

"I met him when I was in eleventh grade, then we saw each other during college."

"Did you love him?" Allie asked.

"Uh huh."

As if! Margaret thought. It had driven her nuts how casual Diana was, how she toyed with Jerome and took him for granted. Apparently Diana remembered it differently. The sight of Jerome rendered her features young and sweet, and she gazed at him wistfully, the way Margaret had gazed at the girls when they were babies, when she was both happy and pained to see them getting bigger.

"I loved him a lot more than I understood at the time," Diana said.

As if picking up on Diana's nostalgia—he wouldn't pick up on Margaret's, he'd never picked up on any of her feelings—he suddenly stared in their direction. Diana waved, but in an uncharacteristically small way, and he didn't respond. She'd been up on her toes, but sank back down when he turned away again. "I guess he didn't see me," she said. "I wonder what he thinks of me now?"

Typical, Margaret thought with great disgust. Diana didn't even consider that he might not recognize her, and she assumed she was on his mind. What would it be like to be so sure of oneself?

"Do you think I should go talk to him?" Diana asked.

"I thought you were here for the girls."

"It would only take a minute."

Margaret shrugged. "Do what you want." You will anyway, she thought darkly.

She couldn't stand watching Diana trying to make up her mind whether or not to reopen old wounds so she turned her attention to her handbag and the girls' tickets. She'd had them in her desk for the past two weeks and had checked them daily. She'd always been like that: the person chosen to take the roll call, keep the score, be the treasurer. Someone had to. The tickets were there, of course, between her checkbook and wallet. She pulled them out and held them in her hand.

"Maybe if I talk to him I could finally get some closure on this," said Diana.

"Whatever," Margaret said, steeling herself for the old, painful picture of Jerome and Diana together, their heads bent close. "Allie, help me with the suitcase, will you?"

The girls hovered near her as she handed in their tickets and made the final arrangements for their flying unescorted. For a moment she forgot all about Jerome and thought only of the children, the safety of the children, and of how empty their bedrooms would be for the next couple of weeks, how still the house. This was where her proper suit came in handy, and her proper tone of voice. The man behind the counter was both deferential and protective. When she was all set, she turned around and saw the girls—all three of them— watching Jerome Strauss disappear into a spidery leg of the terminal.

"So you decided not to accost the poor man after all?" Margaret said.

"I'll find him. I just need a few minutes, to think of what I want to say."

"Maybe you need a cigarette to steady your nerves," Evie said.

"See the kind of example you set?" Margaret accused Diana. She turned to the girls. "No one ever needs a cig- arette for any reason. We'll go get something to eat."

"Speaking of reasons—there's got to be a reason why Jerome and I are here, together, now," Diana said.

"I'd hardly say you're here together."

"Maybe not literally, but you've got to admit it's an amazing coincidence. I didn't see a ring on his finger, did you?"

Margaret didn't answer. She didn't want to admit she'd looked.

"Don't get anything heavy," Margaret said. They were in line in the cafeteria. "Just a salad or some soup. The flight can be hard on your stomach."

"Oh, let them have whatever they want," Diana said. "This is a special occasion."

The girls looked at Margaret uncertainly.

"All right. Within reason. I'm sure your father will let you eat anything you want anyway." She heard the harshness in her voice, but she couldn't help it. She was still nonplussed by how afraid the children had been to walk through the security checkpoint. Diana was the one who figured out what was bothering them. She guessed that they were under the sway of the schoolyard wisdom that predicted the metal hooks in their bras would set off the alarms on the metal-detector gates. They were both in training bras, way before Margaret would have thought them necessary, but for once, she'd given in to their pleas for conformity; they claimed all their friends had them, and that the boys were merciless to those who didn't. In her day, it had been the other way around, but she took their word for it. What harm could it do? She hoped that allowing them to wear bras would be her latest triumph in reverse psychology; they would feel secure, at one with the other girls, which might preserve their childhoods a bit longer.

When they didn't set off a slew of alarms, they slumped with relief. Evie became a little girl again, smiling and curling her fingers into triumphant fists, while Allie grabbed her knapsack off the conveyor belt, located her hairbrush and whipped it fiercely through her hair. Margaret wanted to hug them but restrained herself. Diana, though, had thrown her arms around them both and made a few intimate, jokey remarks about the trials of being a woman that they hadn't minded at all.

"Wow," Diana said as she watched the girls choose yogurts and rolls. She looked at Margaret. "You've certainly got them well trained." She turned to Allie and Evie. "Eat like that and you'll be beautiful forever."

They smiled hopefully up at their aunt. Diana poured two cups of coffee while Margaret paid for everything. When they'd commandeered a vacant table, Evie used a napkin to brush the crumbs left by the previous occupants into her hand. Diana sat down, shook her arms out of her coat, and took a bracing swig of her coffee. "That's better. God. I really thought I was going to fall on the floor right there."

Margaret drummed her fingertips against her mug. "That would've been just what I needed."

"He looked cute, didn't he?" Diana fished.

"You sound like a teenager."

"Hey, you were a teenager once upon a time yourself. At least biologically. Although I have to say it didn't seem to make much of an impression on you."

"I bet she was the same as she is now, right?" Allie said.

"You got it. A Girl Scout all the way."

"At least I wasn't insanely boy crazy like some people I know."

"This sounds *good*." Allie rubbed her hands and

scrunched up her face in a typically exaggerated performance while Evie merely widened her eyes. In spite of the difference in pitch, they were equally interested. "Tell," Allie said.

"It was truly sickening," Margaret began. "All Diana talked about were boys, boys, boys, all day, all night. As you would say, Allie, yuck city."

"But I wasn't a shrinking violet. You can't accuse me of that," Diana said.

The girls burst out laughing.

"What's so funny?" Diana asked.

"A shrinking violet," Allie giggled.

"I think that's an expression way before their time," Margaret teased.

Diana grimaced. "Are you calling me old?"

"Did I say that?"

"At least I don't act old. Not like some people I know." Diana pointed to Margaret under cover of her palm, making the girls laugh again.

"Ahem," Margaret said, playing along. "Weren't we talking about Aunt Diana?"

"Right!" Evie said. "What did she do?"

Margaret leaned closer to the table. The girls instinctively copied her, encouraging her confidence.

"She always had a crush on one boy or another. I think the first one was Tommy Duffy. That was fourth grade, right, Di?"

"Tommy Duffy," Diana said dreamily. "He stole a bracelet from his mother and gave it to me."

"How romantic," Margaret drawled. The girls loved sarcasm, and she didn't mind pandering once in a while. They giggled right on cue. "Then, if memory serves, there was Chauncey Biddle."

"Chauncey!" the girls shrieked.

"If you'd seen how cute he was, you would have learned to ignore the name, too," Diana said with mock defensiveness.

"Then who?" Evie asked.

"I think that brings us to Billy Bell," said Diana. "He was a surfer."

"A New Jersey surfer," Margaret amended.

"What's that?" Allie asked.

"Never mind," Diana said. "Your mother's just jealous. Billy was very blond, very skinny, very tough. I used to follow him around and he'd pretend he didn't see me until all of his friends peeled off to their houses or wherever. Then, when he was sure no one was looking, we'd kiss. After him I met Blair Warren. . . ."

Diana took over, to the girls' delight, embellishing the stories way beyond Margaret's bald recitation of names. And stories they were, for half of Diana's fun had been to describe the blow-by-blow, the he-said-I-said, and to show around her love letters. When Margaret was sixteen, she'd written in her diary one night that if she died right then, the life that passed before her eyes would be a series of scenes of Diana appearing in the doorway of Margaret's bedroom, saying she just had to talk about some boy or another or she'd faint! Diana was always in love, full of schemes and wishes, and went back and forth between the two, as if they were of equal strategic value. She couldn't understand why Margaret didn't try harder to attract the opposite sex and took it upon herself to instruct Margaret on every tip garnered from the teen magazines she bought after school with her baby-sitting money. Want a wide-eyed look? Draw extra lashes beneath your lower lid. A pouty mouth? Put a dab of concealer in the center of your lower lip. Enhance your bosom? Wear ruffles!

Diana still followed such advice. Just recently she'd come across a reminder that keeping the muscles around her mouth as still as possible could forestall the development of laugh lines and decided it was time she paid attention. For a few days afterward she ate like one of those self-conscious aging beauties who manage to slide their food off their fork, chew it and swallow it, all with their faces in utter repose. But this was one trick that eluded Diana; she looked stiff as a robot and about as attractive. "You'd better check that out in a mirror before you make it a permanent part of your reper-toire," Margaret had advised. Diana said plastic surgery would take care of the problem anyway.

Margaret witnessed Diana's adventures and heart-breaks and, in the manner of sisters, carved out an op-posing identity for herself. She had a reputation for reliability and decided her best course would be to ex-

pand on that and similar qualities. She'd done everything she could to make herself immune to boy craziness, which was easy after she met Jerome, and knew
she'd never love anyone but him. She thought she'd
never marry when, just as she was about to go to law
school, she met Duncan Abbott. Diana had always
thought it funny that he'd picked Margaret up in a museum.

"He knew exactly where to find a girl like you," she
said.

None of his lines had been particularly good, but his
interest was clear though appropriately restrained.
Their courtship was equally fathomable. Nothing he
did disqualified him, and he was straightforward about
his desire for children, a longing she shared. There were
even moments when she adored him. Over time, she
compared him less and less frequently to Jerome.

One day she realized she was going to plunge ahead
with him, so there was no point struggling against the
inevitable. She, who had always had some sort of job
since she was nine years old, even accepted that he had
family money of a magnitude that he didn't have to
work and didn't. Nor did she—terrible, terrible mistake. At least she could make up for that now. She was
going to start law school in the fall and go ahead with a
career, better late than never. She couldn't do a thing
about her bad judgment over Duncan—except raise the
girls to be as unlike him as possible.

. . .

"And then, of course, there were the Beatles," Diana was saying.

The girls looked at each other and shrieked.

"You mean you were one of those Beatle nuts?" Allie winced. Evie clapped her hand over her mouth and bounced up and down.

"A Beatle*maniac*," Margaret instructed.

"Really? How about Mom?" The girls looked at Margaret.

"No way," said Diana. "Can you really imagine her getting carried away like that? No, she didn't fall in love with them. In fact, one night when I was driving her crazy playing the same record over and over—"

" 'Day Tripper,' " Margaret grimaced. "Aunt Diana destroyed that song for me."

"Allie does that to me!" Evie said. "She made me hate Madonna."

Diana was unperturbed. "Well then you'll be glad to know that Margaret got her revenge. She made lists of all the girls we knew, divided onto four pages, with the names of each of the Beatles at the top. Then she told me what it revealed about each of our friends that they liked a particular Beatle the best. It was scary, because she was right, at least for the most part. How did that go again, Marg?"

"Oh, I don't know." Margaret glanced at her watch. They had plenty of time, really.

"Of course you do. Start with John."

"John. All right." She paused and automatically

folded her napkin as she gathered her thoughts. "He was the coolest one, and the girls who liked him were cool, too. They usually wanted to be artists and were the first to start smoking."

Diana nodded. "You see? She remembers. Do Paul."

"The girls who liked him were the ones who dotted their i's with little hearts and said aw! whenever they saw a puppy and never had to go on a diet because they never went off of one. They thought they deserved the cutest boyfriends."

Diana slapped the table happily. "Right! And the Ringo fans knew they wanted to be mothers when they grew up," Diana said. "They were goody-goodies who went caroling at nursing homes and practiced their posture by walking with dictionaries on their heads. Recognize anyone?" she said mischievously.

"Mom!" the girls said, and Margaret didn't deny it.

"One-two-three-four-five-six-seven-eight-nine-ten you owe me a Coke!" Allie looked pleased with herself.

"Remind me to get one for you in California." Evie could be droll when she wanted to.

"And then there were the girls who liked George," Margaret said. "They were imaginative and very romantic. They sat in their bedrooms writing poetry by candlelight and went for long walks in the rain. They tended to marry the wrong person."

"Who did you like, Aunt Diana?" Evie asked.

"George." Diana shook her head. "It's all true, except I never got married."

"Why didn't you marry that guy we just saw?" Allie asked.

"Jerome. Good question. At the time, I thought there were probably better guys out there, and I shouldn't get tied down so early on. But as it turned out, sometimes you meet the best one first." Diana fiddled with her armful of silver bracelets. "Now I really do need a cig."

"Funny. You've never said a word about him since then." Margaret pushed her coffee to the center of the table.

"I'm saying it now. I made a big mistake. Now I'm going to go find some scuzzy corner of this damn place where people are still allowed to smoke. If you're not here when I get back I'll meet you at the gate."

She's going to look for him, Margaret thought.

"What if she can't find us?" Evie asked.

"She will," Margaret said automatically.

Evie didn't look convinced. Margaret thought that if Diana made this situation worse for them, she'd never speak to her again.

In the departure lounge, the girls immediately grabbed a row of seats by the window and settled in, as if they were going to be there forever. Margaret tried to read, but she couldn't concentrate. "How about a game of Rummy 500?" She located the deck of cards in the bag. Allie grabbed it and began to shuffle.

Evie raised her hand, as if she were in school. "May I deal?"

"I'm dealing," Allie said. If ever there was a person who instinctively understood that possession was nine-tenths of the law, it was Allie.

Margaret settled the matter by saying they'd take turns.

"Diana must have smoked a whole pack by now." Allie organized her hand efficiently, her cards snapping.

"She's probably in one of the shops," Margaret said.

"Maybe she found Jerome again and they're still in love!" Evie's face was bright, shining from within.

Margaret frowned. "I doubt it."

"Like you doubt that you and Daddy could get back together again," Evie said.

"Right. That's very doubtful."

"You really don't love Daddy anymore? Not even a little bit?" Allie asked.

I can't think why I would, Margaret thought. "I'm afraid not, honey." She had promised herself she wouldn't lie to them about this.

"Do you think he's changed since the last time we saw him?" Evie asked.

"I hope so!" Margaret said automatically and laughed. But Evie just stared intently at her cards, and Allie blushed.

"I'm sorry. That was a bad joke," Margaret said. "So what do you think you want to see in Los Angeles?"

"Nothing," Evie said.

"Ditto," said Allie.

It was small of her, she knew, but Margaret was

pleased that the girls weren't projecting much fun. "The beaches are supposed to be nice."

"Daddy said he would take us to Disneyland," Evie said neutrally. She was holding the lead and growing more serious with each hand she won, tamping down her excitement and hedging her bets in case her luck ran out. It bothered Margaret to see this cautiousness, and she tried to offer subdued encouragement. Subdued, because she never knew which girl to root for. Allie was so able and so competitive that Margaret often neglected to cheer her on, but she identified with mild Evie. Margaret had been raised to be a good loser—at her school, the best sportsmanship award had always been given to the girl who was literally the best sport rather than the best athlete—but was it right to impose this view on her daughter? Especially as it would be such a struggle for Allie to learn, a denial of her nature.

Yet Margaret was glad to see Evie winning. It was so rare that she could do anything tangibly better than her sister. Her strongest point was a deep moral acuity, but who knew if the world would honor that? Margaret would never forget an incident that had taken place when Evie was eight. A friend of Margaret's was describing her rather brutal efforts to train her dog. "I would never hit a dog," Evie told Margaret later, her smooth forehead furrowed with concern. "It would be like if I went to Europe and everyone hit me when I couldn't understand what they were saying." It was a clear, sharp perception that left Margaret in awe.

"Earth to Mom, earth to Mom, where are you?" Allie asked.

Margaret grew serious. "Remember I'm going to call you at seven o'clock, California time. Don't let your father take you anywhere before I talk to you and know you got there safely."

They nodded.

"And you can always call me. Collect, if you need to."

Allie picked a card and laid down her hand.

"Congratulations, Al," Evie said.

Allie shrugged. "It was like I got great cards. Anyway, I have to go to the bathroom." She began to walk off.

"Wait a minute," Margaret said. "We're coming with you."

Allie turned around. "Oh, I can go by myself."

Her tone was so reasonable that for a moment Margaret considered it. She wanted to stay close to the gate; she was afraid of having their tickets given away to standby passengers. Then she came to her senses.

"No, you can't."

"Mom," Allie wheedled.

"No." Margaret stood up decisively and inured herself to Allie's ongoing pleas that included the people around them and begged for the sympathy of reasonable minds. Well, I'm not reasonable, Margaret thought, not when it comes to the prospect of young girls being allowed to wander the corridors of airports on their own. Or to look at it another way, she was utterly reasonable in the face of all the potential craziness out there. She didn't want to explain this angle on reasonableness to Allie, however; the truth was the substance of night-mares, so she let her strictness be interpreted as one of her own inexplicable quirks. If the girls were properly policed now, with luck, soon enough, they'd know how to protect themselves. It hurt to have Allie throw sullen glances her way as she tried to convince strangers to align themselves against her, but someone had to be the adult. She shuddered to think how Duncan would handle such instances; it was too disturbing to contemplate; she pushed it out of her mind.

Then Evie wanted to remain behind to wait for Diana. She was worried that they wouldn't find her again.

"We're all going together," Margaret said, her tone accepting no negotiation. Then her hope broke through; perhaps, as they passed by other gates, she'd see Jerome.

"What about our stuff?" Allie asked.

The three of them looked at the children's array of things, which lay used and scattered around their seats as at the end of a day of play.

"I'll watch everything for you," offered a man who had been sitting across from them for quite some time.

"No, thanks," Allie said coolly and hastily packed up. It depressed Margaret to see that the girls understood how to watch over their property better than they knew how to protect themselves. They stuck close to her until they had turned the corner. Then they stepped ahead and strode along the shiny floor together, ignoring her watchful presence, pretending they were free.

. . .

The bathroom smelled of a combination of disinfectant, cigarettes, and stale perfume. A thin man was desultorily swabbing the floors with a frayed gray mop while a chestnut-skinned woman fed hot dog chunks to an exhausted child who lay on the plank that served as a changing table. Allie and Evie, subdued by the ugly atmosphere, shuffled wordlessly toward the stalls, casting glances at Margaret to make sure she would be standing guard. She felt a flash of satisfaction at their need. In her mind, she challenged their father to match this. He'd never changed a diaper, never taken them to school, never done any of the scut work unless other people were around whom he might be able to snow into thinking he was a good father.

It had amazed her when he pushed for a very precise visitation schedule; she'd imagined he wouldn't care, particularly as the girls had reported that he had a girlfriend in tow the last time he met them for a visit in the city, someone closer to their age than hers, the descriptions of whom had ranged from okay to cool. The children did not like to talk about the girlfriend; they had absorbed enough of the culture to know that younger women had more currency than did mothers with crinkly lines around their eyes, and they did not want to make Margaret jealous. She *was* jealous, but not in the way they thought. She was jealous that this stranger would be with her children when she couldn't be.

She looked at the mirror, dismayed at what Jerome

would see if she found him. She saw a sweet-looking woman in her late thirties who seemed to wither beneath even her own scrutiny. She pulled out her lipstick and did what she could. She still looked haggard, she thought, and divorced, but when the girls came out of the stalls, Evie's eyes lit up at the effort she'd made, which would have to do.

"That's an old lady color," Allie said. "Can I get a magazine to read on the plane?"

"I think you look pretty, Mom. I need some gum so my ears won't pop," said Evie.

Margaret looked at herself in the mirror and saw that the children had spoken true to type: Allie was right and Evie was considerate.

"If you promise you'll spit it out as soon as the take-off is over," she said.

She wiped away the lipstick with a piece of paper towel and surreptitiously loosened a few strands of hair from her ponytail. Breezy, she decided as she took a quick last look at herself. Drab is more like it, she thought as they walked back out to the concourse.

She reminded herself that it wouldn't matter either way.

Even among the restless travelers Diana created a stir as she loped into the newsstand, her hair billowing. Just as she entered, the first boarding call for the girls' flight was announced, but she didn't seem to notice. She looked driven and shell-shocked and self-absorbed.

Damn, Margaret thought as she watched the spectacle of Diana unself-consciously commandeering the attention of everyone in the shop.

Diana spotted her and rushed over.

"You talked to him," Margaret said.

Diana slowly began to smile.

"Well?" Margaret heard herself sound shrill.

"His plane is delayed for an hour. I'm going to meet him for a drink."

"How are you going to get home then?"

"You're going to come have a drink with me." Diana was flirting already, warming up.

"No way."

"Yes way. Come on, Marg. You always liked him."

"That has nothing to do with it, Diana."

"What's the problem, then?"

Margaret gave an exasperated shrug.

"What? What?" Diana said.

"The problem is that today isn't about you. We're not here for you and your love life." The girls had spotted them together and were walking over. Margaret lowered her voice. "Just focus on the girls for five minutes, will you?"

"Aunt Diana!" Evie gave Diana a hug, as if they'd been separated for months.

"You saw him again, didn't you?" Allie said knowingly.

Diana grinned.

"What happened?"

"Nothing—yet!" Diana said. She told Allie about the "date" she'd made.

"He's not married?" Margaret asked pointedly.

Diana shrugged. "He is. I established that right away. But I got the feeling he isn't very happy."

Of course you did, Margaret thought.

"Can I have this one, Mom?" Allie asked, proffering a copy of *Mademoiselle.*

Margaret scanned the table of contents. Careers and cramps, as usual. "I guess so," she said. Any other response might lead to a fight, and it was no time for a fight.

"Why isn't he happy?" Evie asked, taking Diana's hand.

"That's what I plan to find out."

"Would you stop filling their heads with this garbage?" Margaret said.

"I'm just trying to lighten things up a little bit. Jeez!"

"What a classy way you have of doing it," Margaret said coldly.

Diana shook her head. "Anyone want some candy?" she said and led the children over to the cash register, leaving Margaret alone to wonder at the florid covers of the paperbacks.

"We have to pick up the pace," Margaret said. "It's going to take us a few minutes to get back to the gate."

"I don't want to go," Evie said. "Please, Mommy, let me stay home."

Great, Margaret thought. Diana had stimulated them, pierced the calm; now they'd balk. And she wouldn't think she'd played any part in their unwillingness. She walked alongside them, perusing her own thoughts, a small, faraway smile on her lips.

"That can't happen, Evie. The judge ordered this visit."

"But can't you explain to him that we want to stay home?" Allie said. She had her arms crossed over her chest, looking just like Duncan even as she struggled against seeing him.

"No," Margaret said. "I can't. I know you're nervous," Margaret soothed, "but you'll be fine. He's your father, remember."

"That's the problem," Evie said. "I hardly remember him."

Their helplessness was palpable and entered Margaret at every pore. As the children's flight was called again, she felt her nerves gather into a hard, swollen lump in her throat, an ice cube swallowed whole. She watched herself from an unfrequented place so deep inside that it may as well have been the point of view of a stranger. There, she wanted to run away with the children, to hold on to them with a desperate ferocity that would vanquish laws and agreements and everyone else's rights. Instead, she coaxed them down the corridor, a hand on each of their backs, pushing, pushing, all the while enveloped in a rush of raw feeling that made her heart seem to expand, then stop.

The sensation was by now familiar, yet it still over-
whelmed; for a second or five or ten she was suspended
in a parallel universe with a very real sense that she
might not return to this one unless she willed herself to
do so. It seemed up to her to get her system working
again by reminding herself not to worry, that she knew
what was happening and it was nothing serious. It was
just that very ordinary feeling she had several times a
day when she was utterly taken up with her children;
seeing them; thinking of them; hearing their voices so
clearly that every other sound was muted. It's only that,
she reminded herself, thankful that she had an explanation for such a cataclysmic physical event. Otherwise, if
her heart were as disturbed, she would think she was
dying.

"I'll talk to you tonight," she said as they reached
the gate.

"Are you sure Daddy knows when to meet us?" Evie
asked. "What do we do if we get there and he's not
there?"

"Someone from the airline will be with you until he
meets you. If anything goes wrong, just call me. But you
have nothing to worry about."

"I think I might have told him we were coming tomorrow," Allie said.

"He knows it's today," Margaret said firmly.

"Please don't make me go," Evie said. She squeezed
Margaret's hand and bounced gently up and down, then
let go and clung to Diana. "I want to stay home!"

"Hey," Diana said. "Did I ever tell you what happened on the day you guys were born?"

"We weren't born on the same day," Allie said.

"I mean the days, wise guy, the days. Both times your dad called me from the hospital and said 'I have the most gorgeous baby girl in the world right here who needs the most beautiful name. Got any ideas?' "

"You mean you named us?" Evie asked.

"No, no. I made a few suggestions. Your dad chose the names. I think he did a pretty good job, don't you?"

"You're just trying to make us feel better," Allie accused, but with no malice.

"Your dad loves you," Diana said. "He's your dad, the one and only."

The girls leaned on her and all three of them cried. Margaret stood by and watched for what she felt was a decent interlude. Then she stepped forward and took command.

"We have to say good-bye now, girls." She could barely breathe.

Sniffling, they all straightened up.

"Write me a postcard," Diana said. Like a kid, she wiped her eyes on her palms. Margaret fought for the composure to get through the next few minutes.

A flight attendant approached. "You're the Abbott girls? Are you ready?"

"I'm their mother," Margaret said.

The woman lay a soft, consoling hand on Margaret's arm. "Make it brief. It's easier for everyone that way."

Then she took a few steps backward, just enough to suggest she understood the concept of privacy but not enough to provide it. Margaret tried to ignore her. She hugged and kissed them quickly, as per instruction, and then stepped back in favor of the lurking stewardess. The girls hoisted their backpacks onto their shoulders with resigned expressions on their faces that made them look eerily middle-aged.

Margaret leaned against the cold glass, her eyes fixed on the runway, waving stubbornly at the inscrutable pewter-colored windows of the plane long after there was any chance that the girls might see her. As it lifted into the air, Margaret imagined them chewing their gum, gradually loosening their tight, anxious grip on the arms of their seats. She turned around. Diana was standing behind her.

"What's wrong?" Margaret said automatically.

"I'm sorry, Marg. It's awful, truly it is."

Margaret looked back at the disappearing jet. It was just heading into the clouds and the swirling snow was obliterating the smoky trail it had drawn in its wake. It had snowed the day she and Duncan got married. He had surprised her with a sapphire guard ring, which he guided over her knuckles along with the wedding band. Something blue, he said aloud, right during the cere-mony. Her heart had squeezed small as a sponge, then puffed back up with all the life she had in her. She had loved him when they married. The plane disappeared completely but she kept her palms pressed against the cold windows for a few moments more. She had loved him on many occasions, more genuinely than she'd ever admitted either to herself or to him. Part of her still did, albeit a small, maverick aspect of her heart that she found incomprehensible and would rather have done without. She did not know how to reconcile that residual affection with all the sorrow.

"I guess we might as well go," she said.

"Jerome's waiting in the VIP lounge. Come have a drink with him."

Margaret stared resolutely out the window, enveloped in the shroud of separation. The clouds were thick, low, and utterly obscuring. Flurries swirled up off the runway in blustery cones that raced across the ground for a few dizzying yards before imploding into miniature blizzards. The departing planes disappeared into the cloud bank upon liftoff; the girls' was long gone.

"Maybe I shouldn't have let them go. It really is nasty out there."

"They'll be fine. If the plane were going to crash, you'd have sensed it." Diana touched her shoulder. "You must be exhausted."

Margaret registered the word and immediately succumbed to it. "Yes, I am."

Bed. Sleep. Oblivion. Snow piled on the windows, snow and the quiet of it. She'd have to know the girls were safe before she could rest, though. She'd have to wait up.

"I'll drive you home," Diana offered.

"What about Jerome?"

"We'll stop and tell him we have to go."

"All right."

But when they got to the lounge she said she had to go to the ladies' room. In the stall she rested her elbows on her knees for a moment, then went to the sink and pressed her face with a wet paper towel.

"Ready?" Diana said, startling her.

"That was fast."

"He wasn't there." She looked . . . not young.

"Oh well," Margaret said. "You could have a drink at my house."

"That's okay. I want to go back to sleep myself."

Sure enough, as soon as they got in the car, Diana dropped off. Margaret watched a plane climb the sky and wondered if it was Jerome's. The girls were probably arguing over whether or not to pull the shade against the sudden sun. Evie would want to look out at the sky and Allie would be forced by the logic of their preferences to give up her window seat. There would be other little squabbles and negotiations all through the flight, right up until they walked along the cordoned passageway to meet their father. At that moment they would close ranks and support each other, at least until they knew where they stood with the rest of the world. Thank God they had each other.

"What are you thinking about?" Diana asked.

"Duncan." It just came out.

"He's a jerk." In an instant, Diana was asleep again.

The girls called at ten sharp.

"There was a really gross man next to us on the plane, Mom," Allie reported. "His shirt kept coming untucked, and you could see his hairy butt."

"Daddy told us we look like teenagers," Evie said.

As she hung up, Margaret felt her heart twist. Silent sound, vivid absence, the ache of adoration and devotion in every cell of her body; she missed her girls. She called Diana and went up to bed—but when she couldn't sleep, she made a search of the attic, found her passionate diaries, and burned them in the fieldstone fireplace.

Home

THE LONG, narrow room was divided neatly in half by a wooden shelf, on one side of which was a sofa and on the other, a bed, creating "areas" for living and sleeping. Lil Pepper surveyed it in an instant, then headed for the door. She assumed the others would follow her, but when she turned around, no one had moved. Instead, the three of them stood in a tense row, watching her with a rapt attention that made her feel as though there was someone else behind her at whom they were really looking.

"They" were her daughter, Charlotte; Charlotte's husband, Jack; and a Mrs. Stafford, who had been with them for the past hour and a half as they settled Lil's husband, Gordon, in the care center two floors below. Who is she exactly? Lil wondered, but no one ever said; and eventually it was too late to ask without seeming rude or foolish. Clearly Mrs. Stafford had something to do with this place—Lil let it go at that. It didn't really matter to her so much anymore who people were.

"This is smaller than the room we saw in July," Charlotte said, "but you'll move to a bigger one with Daddy as soon as he finishes his physical therapy."

Lil felt herself turn toward Charlotte as if turning in the direction of a loud noise she couldn't quite decipher. Her mouth went slack, and she willfully closed it again, all with the heavy, bewildering sense of slow motion she'd had more and more lately. She could not remember having been here in July.

"Normally this wing is more expensive," Mrs. Stafford said, lowering her voice a notch when she spoke about money, "but we're not going to bother about that. We like to show extra consideration to our long-term residents."

"Thank you," Charlotte said. She glanced at Lil in much the same way that Lil used to glance at her, a parental, directive look meant to prompt a mannerly response. Lil was steadied by it.

"It's nice," she said perfunctorily. Polite but neutral.

Mrs. Stafford came closer, breaking into a smile that gave Lil a peculiar feeling. Gordon always said that a bare-toothed smile was a sign of aggression. It was the kind of remark he made that she routinely ignored, but that had penetrated nevertheless. Over the years, she had reluctantly come to take notice of the characteristics he found most objectionable in the public at large: a flat back of the head, a sagging pair of narrow shoulders, the slight overbite he associated with halitosis. He could perfectly happily watch television with the sound off just to spot these physical idiosyncrasies, from which he was able to extrapolate the essence of a person's limitations of spirit, particularly those of second-rate television actors.

It was a game that had always amused the children, but Lil had found it disquieting and slightly mean. It was one of those habits of his for which she had been a foil rather than an audience. She had never subscribed to his theories, but she found herself riffling through the catalog of them in her mind as this woman's big smile filled her with dread.

"I'm glad you like it. Now before you settle in, let me show you how to get to the dining room from here," Mrs. Stafford said. She stretched her hand out toward Lil, palm down, as if to grab her by the wrist. Lil crossed her arms. The handle of her black leather bag slipped along the sleeve of her suit until it dangled from her elbow.

"That's all right," Lil said.

"Oh, it's no bother. It's my job." Again, the discomfiting grin. "You're one of the lucky ones, Mrs. Pepper. The dining room and the library are both on this floor."

"Well, I for one would like to see it," Charlotte said. She came up from behind Lil and hugged her around the shoulders. "I wish there were places like this for people our age. Don't you, Jack?"

Lil couldn't see Jack, but she imagined he was nodding. He would nod whether or not he really wanted to live in a place like this, to back up Charlotte. He loved her; Lil was grateful. Charlotte was her youngest, a late-life accident that turned out to be a gift, and her only daughter. She'd grown up to be a bright, sweet, pretty woman, girlish even now in her mid-thirties. Lil didn't believe in favorites, but it was only natural to feel more of an affinity for certain people than others—Charlotte was the one of her offspring with whom she felt closest.

It wasn't that they got along so well. They'd had their moments, to be sure, especially when Charlotte was a teenager and their disagreements had been so frequent that they took on a discernible pattern. Charlotte would say something provocative; Lil would venture that Charlotte didn't really mean that; Charlotte would charge that Lil was denying her "personhood" and cry in a muffled, embarrassed, frustrated way until whatever storm that assailed her had passed, making way for a bright, clear calm. Then they would both apologize and their real talk would begin.

"I know it's not you who is denying my personhood, Ma," Charlotte had said once, "but I do feel it being denied, and it frightens me."

Lil had never forgotten that remark, for it so accurately expressed a feeling she'd long had. She'd thought about it often since then and had finally decided it was the feeling the women's liberation movement was trying to address—that feeling she'd had since she was a small girl, of being not quite visible.

It was a sensation that came and went. There were certainly people and situations and places that brought her out to a degree that she knew she appeared whole. Charlotte could usually be counted on to have this effect. Lil could still bring to mind the exact sound of Charlotte's heavy Abercrombie shoes—required for school—clomping up the stairs to the bedroom, where she sat on the sofa and asked all kinds of questions while Lil dressed for dinner. How do you know when you're in love? How do you decide where everyone will sit at a dinner party? Do you really believe in God?

Lil looked up at Charlotte now, searching for some trace of the old, almost conspiratorial connection that used to make Lil feel so vivid and necessary, but when their eyes met, Charlotte gave a weak smile that hollowed Lil out. Finally she understood. She was being put away; she had no choice in the matter; Charlotte had been designated by the family to do the dirty work, to soften the blow, just as a few years earlier Charlotte had been the one forced to take her car keys away from her when it was decided Lil shouldn't drive anymore. Gordon couldn't help her. No, worse: Gordon knew. So, Lil thought, this is it.

For a single moment she accepted the situation and had the kind of prosaic thought that gains weight in the timing of its application—that her time had come, as it had come to many before her and would to many again. Then she felt a split second of peace, during which she continued to make sense of what was happening in the odd, lofty way that came upon her every once in a while and made her wonder about herself. She thought with an amused clarity that her ingrained sense of her own insignificance was finally coming in handy, enabling her to accept being blown where the wind took her, like a piece of dandelion fluff.

"All right," she said. "I'll look around."

Charlotte hugged her again, and with a soft, pincer-like motion down by her side that was meant to be un-noticeable, she beckoned her husband to follow her. He came up on the other side of Lil and applied a discreet pressure to her elbow, steering her out the door and along the whispering corridor. Lil allowed them to guide her, her will-less limbs feeling loose as a mari-onette's.

"Here's the main dining room," Mrs. Stafford said. She pushed both the doors open at once, walked a few steps into the empty room, and turned in triumph, as if she were a cicerone in a shrine. She babbled on about the fun to be had there, and Lil tried to listen with an open mind, telling herself it could be true. She had al-ways enjoyed her club, after all, had liked eating down-stairs before bridge with a table full of friends, among tables full of other friends, everyone in neat wool suits. As Charlotte and Jack perused the menu for the week and oohed and aahed over the choices, Lil imagined eat-ing at one of the large tables by the wall of windows. She pictured the tables set with pink linen and fragrant centerpieces like a wedding reception.

"Think of all the new friends you'll make," Charlotte was saying. "In no time you'll be the most popular person, like you are everywhere you go. She's a very good bridge player," she told Mrs. Stafford.

"We have our own league here. You just let me know when you're ready, and I'll get you all signed up." Mrs. Stafford spoke so loudly that it was all Lil could do not to step backward, away from the thunder. "I'm going to leave you now to explore on your own. I'm very pleased to meet you, and I know you'll love it once you get used to it. All our residents do."

She shook Lil's hand. Did the residents really love it, or did they just become resigned? Lil wondered. If Gordon had been with her, he would have shot her a glance to show what a horse's ass he thought this Mrs. Stafford was, even as he gave the woman a warm send-off, complete with one of his unctuous smiles. Lil looked to Charlotte and Jack for a confirmation of her judgment, but Charlotte was in a huddle with the woman, and Jack—well, for a moment he appeared about to say something, but he quickly became neutral and composed again, a human Switzerland.

"I think I should check on Gordon now," Lil said when the three of them were alone.

"Good idea!" Charlotte nodded rapidly. "I want to make sure you know how to get to his room."

They walked for some time. The halls were tweedy and vacuous, with framed posters rather than windows lining the walls. Jack kept looking over at her apprehensively. He sees it for what it is, Lil thought, no matter what he pretends.

"Are you paying attention, Mother? Remember, you'll turn left at the picture of the parrots and keep going until you get to the elevator."

Lil made the turn and continued on. Suddenly there was a window. It opened onto a courtyard, and a little room full of plants.

"Look," Charlotte said, "a greenhouse. You'll probably want to spend some time in here."

"It's very nice," Lil said. There was no one in the greenhouse, no one anywhere. "Is this where we were going when we left the shore this morning?" she asked.

Charlotte had reached another elevator bank, pushed another button. "Yes."

"I thought we were going home."

Charlotte looked at Jack.

"This is going to be your home now, Ma, remember? We all decided it would be best."

Who decided? Lil wondered. She didn't remember anything about it, but she kept the lapse to herself. The elevator door closed and she stood quietly, obediently, in the fluorescent box, whirring downward, toward Gordon.

The Peppers owned two houses, and a condo in Florida, all bought for a song decades earlier. It was September, when they always moved back to Wynnemoor from their shore house. That was what they had been doing today, or so she thought. It was definitely that time of year. She would have known it just as well without the calendar; the signs were as familiar and her interpretation of them as automatic as her own pulse.

The mass exodus took place right after Labor Day. All that long weekend there were good-byes in the air, graceful, lighthearted fare-thee-wells that eddied among the shingled summer cottages. The breezes that carried everyone's good wishes along were less vigorous than they had been in the middle of the summer, when they were liable to slam doors—always when the children were napping, of course—and rattle the thin old windowpanes.

The windows whistle and chatter like fancy-free men riding the rails.

She'd written that sentence once in the margin of a book. It was a spontaneous thought that both embarrassed and pleased her. She never knew quite what to make of such thoughts. They gave her an odd feeling, as if she were suddenly rushing headlong into the world, connected to everything. (She shuddered now to think of anyone finding that book and seeing the jotting. A horse's ass, indeed.)

On that last weekend of the summer, everyone arrived at the beach a few minutes earlier and stayed a bit longer. For once, the children were allowed to have a Coca-Cola before lunch, a privilege usually reserved for the afternoon, so that it would seem like a treat rather

than a weary accommodation to the long days of instruction and discipline and attempts to rein in the
children's wild energy which, unchecked, might have
carried them straight out to sea. The women sat in low,
wooden beach chairs and talked, their hands busy with
knitting and needlepoint. They spoke more openly on
the final weekend of the summer and paid less attention
to their roles of mother or grandmother, often letting
their charges stay in the water for so long that the children emerged of their own accord and voluntarily approached the adults' circle of chairs, where they stood
shivering and blue-lipped, wrapping their towels
around their nut-brown shoulders, the expression in
their eyes becoming more and more confused when they
didn't inspire the usual concern that they dry off before
they caught cold.

Finally the women put their work down and went
into the ocean all at the same time, laughing at the way
they must have looked in their similar, flowered-cotton
bathing suits. "Who says women don't wear uniforms?"
someone was bound to remark. They may have felt sen-
timental, but they behaved like giddy girls as they
jumped the waves or rode them in. Somewhere along
the way they recaptured the old, long-gone feeling
they'd had before they were married, when they didn't
yet know how they would end up. They were reckless
with hope as they faced the broad horizon, with nothing
lying between them and Africa. After a time a new
mood came over them—it was hard to say what caused

the shift, a lull in the cacophony behind them, perhaps, or a flat, unpromising stretch of sea, or a sense that the amount of time allotted to them for letting themselves go was running out—and they collectively walked back toward the lifeguard stand, their steps heavy with water and their limbs stinging with salt.

The children were waiting for them, strung along the water's edge like a line of police, their stern, disapproving faces causing a flutter of nervous laughter among the women, who for a moment saw themselves two ways at once: as the tough, brave, jaunty types who had run into the water and as the wives and mothers who intuitively knew when it was time to come to their senses, to go home and pack. They exchanged glances and waved casual good-byes, not saying much at the end. Good-bye, see you next year! Cool as soldiers, but carrying their camaraderie with them wherever they went.

The men, too, had their end-of-season rituals. At cocktail parties they could be overheard discussing the same old things, but they lingered a bit longer in each conversation and laughed more appreciatively at each other's jokes. They stood on the wide covered porches in their pale linen jackets, and in subtle, barely discernible ways they touched one another, arm brushing against arm, elbow bumping elbow, as they raised their drinks. On the ride home from the last party, Gordon always said, "Well, that's over with." Lil never replied, knowing he didn't want to talk further about it. She knew he knew she knew what he really meant.

Finally the car would be packed. She put their clothes in garbage bags rather than suitcases, because they were lighter and easier to fit around the other objects in the trunk. Gordon did the arranging in the car, but there was always a moment at the very end when he told her to find a place for one last item while he went back into the house and checked each window, each drawer, each closet for the umpteenth time. On a quiet day, she could hear his footsteps going all the way up to the third floor. Sometimes she spotted his face at the window and, not wanting to intrude on his private moment, she turned away, knowing he was gazing out at the ocean, making one last inventory of the boats.

When she heard him coming back downstairs she got behind the wheel and waited as he gave May, the cleaning woman, last-minute instructions for locking the house. He gave May a bonus, too—Lil never asked how much—then walked out to the garage where he rattled the rusty doorknob. Oddly, this was the image that often came to her when she pictured him: his profile, silhouetted against the unruly growth of trumpet vine and wild rose that ran for two miles between the back of their property and the bay. It was him at his most solitary and exposed. When he joined her again, she always pretended she'd been straightening the glove box and hadn't seen a thing.

In recent years, most of their old friends no longer made the trek to the shore; many were dead. There were fewer parties, and then no parties. The days had a different rhythm. They didn't do as much, eventually even stopped going to the beach, but the time sped by. After Gordon retired, there was no reason to return to "town" so early, and they stayed well into September, when they had their end of the cape virtually to themselves. The light was a rich, buttery yellow and spread across their whole porch at once, a phenomenon they'd never known about before. The golden days, Gordon called them. He sat in a wicker chair with his binoculars, but he couldn't see much. He wondered why no one went fishing anymore, why these days no one was interested in the sea. She never told him that the horizon was dotted with boats, swarming with boats. She brought him a glass of ginger ale and a small bowl of pretzels and kept many of the things she saw, with her perfect eyesight, to herself.

She did not want to ruin it for him. He was the one who really loved the shore, and he had worked hard enough all his life—harder than she could imagine—that she believed he should have what he loved. If she had had her choice, she might rather have gone to other places occasionally. They'd gone to Europe for their honeymoon, an eight-week journey that took them through England, France, Germany, and Switzerland. Gordon had taken her out in a rowboat on Lake Como. In the middle of the lake he stripped, dove in, and swam around naked, smiling and waving up at her, very pleased with himself. She was only nineteen, yet she understood that he was not trying to embarrass her or to show off, but harmlessly demonstrating his exuberance—for their marriage, for life.

She blushed anyway—he was the only man she'd ever seen naked, and the experience was still crushingly new—but she did her best to hide it, feeling that she was at that moment, as she forced herself to gaze at him rolling around in the water like a seal, becoming a wife. She was both growing bigger than she'd thought possible and at the same time growing old. She had been raised to do whatever others wanted her to do and to value how well she could master putting the needs of others before her own. She didn't see anything wrong in this and was taken aback when Charlotte accused her of not "modeling independence."

"You try to be both independent and married to a man like your father," Lil said.

"I would never marry a man like my father," Charlotte replied. And she hadn't. Jack was mild, conciliatory, thoughtful. Occasionally Lil wondered what it would be like to live with a considerate man; but the thought made her feel disloyal and she never dwelled on it for long.

After the ambitious honeymoon trip she assumed that they would continue to travel; but Gordon was content to go back and forward between their houses and, later, spend the winter in Florida, and she hadn't pressed. She supposed that was an area where she could have been more independent. Many of her friends went

without their husbands on the semiluxurious, semiedu-
cational trips sponsored by various museums, and afterward at the bridge table they laughed about their
adventures as if they were wayward college girls. Lil
liked hearing their stories, which were all the more en-
joyable for knowing she would never have those experiences and would therefore never have heard of such
things in any other way.

Would Gordon have let her go? She didn't know—it
had never come up. He'd certainly hated it when their
children went abroad. Lil had never seen him more
bereft than the day they took Charlotte to catch the
boat in New York. She was sailing to England but her
eventual destination was Eastern Europe. "Why?" he
asked over and over as they drove back to Wynnemoor.
"Why would she want to go there when she could have
anything she wants right here?" He said this with no
sense of irony, no awareness that he sounded like one of
those love-it-or-leave-it types whom he always found
slightly spine-tingling in their blind allegiance to the
flag. No; Gordon was serious. He distrusted any passions based on ideas, such as nationalism, but he distrusted other countries more.

"She wants to go there because it's not here," Lil finally said in exasperation. It made about as much sense
as what he was saying, but it stopped him. Not that he
understood. She could still feel his anxiety wafting
through the house whenever he picked up one of the

thin blue envelopes covered with strange stamps that Lil had left out for him on the front table. He had simply learned not to discuss it aloud. But if Lil had decided to go off on a tour of Siena or Machu Picchu or Yorkshire with the museum group, she imagined he would have broken his silence on the subject. As it was, she heard all his objections anyway. His voice was in her. She had married him at nineteen, when her own voice was just a whisper and his a sure, long note that held her as confidently as he held her in his arms when he told her that she was everything he wanted. That, more than anything else, was what kept her home.

Gordon was sitting up eating off a tray when they joined him in his room. Jack pulled a chair next to him for Lil, then perched himself on the bed next to Charlotte. Gordon had always eaten slowly, bending forward over the plate as if he didn't trust himself not to spill down his front or onto his lap. Lil saw him as she'd seen him thousands of times lift the spoon to his lips and tip the soup into his mouth at the same time as he inhaled it with a small hiss. For the amusement of the children, and later the grandchildren, he'd exaggerated the hiss when teaching them their table manners.

"Be sure to make as much noise as possible," he would say, "so your hostess will know you're enjoying the meal."

Then he'd pull his napkin taut between his hands and

saw it back and forth across his entire lower face, which sent his young audiences into gales. Lil had fallen quite naturally into the role of straight man. "Oh, Gordon." Clucking her tongue in disgust.

They brought in a tray of food for her, too, and she ate, although she didn't have much of an appetite. She tried to talk to Gordon about going home, but just as she had his full attention—he'd pushed his tray away and he was leaning forward toward her—a horrible thing happened. The nurse appeared. She was the youngest of the crew from the summer, the one who she'd heard Gordon say had a "good posterior."

That remark had shaken Lil to the core.

"Dad, Sheila has to leave now. She's come to say good-bye to you," Charlotte said.

The nurse advanced.

"Well, my dear," Gordon said, taking her hand.

"I've really enjoyed working for you, Mr. Pepper." The girl's eyes filled as she looked at him.

"Yes, yes," he said.

The girl wiped her cheek. "I better go." She leaned forward, gave him a hug and a kiss, and broke away with an audible sob. She took a few wobbly steps toward the door, then suddenly she was back again. Her white leather purse plummeted to the floor as her arms flung out to her sides. Gordon was engulfed. The girl's jacket rode up in the back exposing a strip of skin above her pants. A gurgling rose from the pairing, a low laugh.

The girl came up smiling. "I'll come see you sometime," she said. Jack handed her her purse and Charlotte walked her back to the door. Lil stared at Gordon.

"What?" he asked.

"I can't believe it," she said.

"Lil." He reached out his hands to her, but she wouldn't take them. "Lil."

"In front of your daughter."

Gordon looked helplessly at Charlotte. Shameless, shameless, Lil thought.

"Mother, don't be silly," Charlotte said. "Sheila was with you all summer. She was just saying good-bye."

Gordon took the Liberty handkerchief from his breast pocket and handed it to her. Automatically she went to take it, but drew away at the last moment. It fluttered to the floor.

"Oh stop it. Stop it," Lil said.

"I think we should go back upstairs for a little while," Charlotte said to Gordon. "You can come up later to see Mother's room."

"All right," Gordon said meekly. He looked up and gave Lil a bashful smile. "Don't be mad at me, my bride."

"Did you know we were coming here?" Lil asked.

She saw Gordon look uneasily at Charlotte.

"Don't do that," Lil said.

"Lil, Lil, Lil," Gordon said.

"I am still a person. You could look at me. You could look at me."

252

Lil walked to the door and stopped next to the bathroom to collect herself. She rarely cried in front of anyone—Gordon was more apt to cry than she—and the
tears scalded. She leaned her eyes against her sleeve and
heard them talking in hushed tones behind her.

"What did I do?" Gordon asked.

"Nothing," Charlotte said. "Mother's tired, that's
all."

"I couldn't care less about Sheila. She's a little girl.
Lil knows me better than that."

"Of course she does. Ma isn't always herself anymore."

"I know, I know. But I can't get used to it."

The bathroom had a pungent, sour smell. Instinctively, Lil backed away from it and huddled in the doorway until Charlotte led her back into the fluorescent-lit
hall, saying she thought Lil could use a nap. They
passed a lounge where a group of young black women in
uniforms was smoking and swaying to the barely audible music coming out of a table radio. Lil pitied them
for a moment, for their rotten jobs, and then realized
that Gordon would be a part of that for them, one of
many, forgotten as soon as they walked out his door.

"Pay attention, Ma. You'll have to do this yourself."

The halls all looked the same to Lil. She waited pas-
sively as Jack turned the key in the lock, but when she
saw the little room again, smelled the thick cloud of air
freshener that couldn't mask the underlying scent of
disinfectant that likewise couldn't cover the sweet,

seeping odor of old age and death, she knew that living here would kill her. Her senses rebelled at the bright decor, aquas and pinks, the colors she and her friends had turned to for amusement when they went to Florida but had never viewed with anything but irony and a shared wink at how they were temporarily escaping from the good taste that was expected of them. But *we* started this, and it was meant to be a joke, she thought, as she looked at the decorative "touches" here and there, the most searing example of which was a series of five Mexican dolls sitting on Plexiglas shelves on the wall. No, she could not live here. She could neither abide this room nor survive its cheerful meanness.

"Charlotte," she said. "Jack. Children. *Please.*"

There was a pause. Then Charlotte stood up.

"I'm sorry, Ma. I should have realized you needed to say good-bye to the house."

Finally they got some sense into their heads and took her home.

As always, everything was exactly the same. Lil thought of the remark Gordon habitually made when they pulled into their driveway at the end of the summer: "God's other country." Charlotte lifted the latch on the heavy garage doors and found the key in its hiding place under a flower pot. She jiggled the back door and banged her shoulder against it.

"Pull the door to you," Lil said.

Charlotte gave it a tug and it swung open.

The house was dark and cool as a chapel, the air thickened with a wet, metallic scent that seeped in continuously from the Pennsylvania fieldstone walls. They all stood in the kitchen while their vision adjusted to the dim light, then pushed through the swinging doors in the pantry—Lil did an inventory at a glance of the hanging cabinets that held her china and glass—and entered the main part of the house.

"Everything's so clean," Jack said.

"As usual," Charlotte replied. "Clean, and in the same place it has been at least since I was born."

Lil overheard and felt a shudder of pride. It's not magic, you know, she imagined herself saying. I did this. Instead, she opened the doors, turning the heavy, iron latchkeys and the brass knobs, first at one end of the hall and then at the other, and a wave of heat rolled in over the faded runner. Heat and light and, in the distance, a child's shriek followed by a sharp slap. The people behind them had recently built a swimming pool. Last March, when the trees between the properties were still bare, she'd seen the piles of flag and the large circle of stakes in the ground, marking off the site. She'd watched these developments for several days before she knew what they meant. How could she know? No one around had ever built a swimming pool before. It wasn't said, but there was a feeling that pools were a bit . . . well, a luxury, at least, that people like themselves wouldn't consider. They were plain people, and anyway, they went away for the summer.

She walked up the stairs and looked out the window hoping to catch a glimpse of the children swimming, but the leaves were too thick, the view obscured. She'd heard the new family had paid over one million dollars for the property. Gordon had had the opportunity to buy that house in 1931 for four thousand dollars. The man who owned it then had lost his money in the crash. He had come to Gordon one afternoon, and the two men had sat in the living room for quite some time. Lil went on an errand, then out for a walk. When she returned the light was fading, but Gordon hadn't turned on the lights. It bothered her to think of their poor neighbor in the darkening room. On her way upstairs to dress for dinner, she had popped in and flicked the switch. She'd thought she'd handled it well until Gordon told her over their cocktail that he'd left the lights off on purpose.

"He was looking for an easy way out. He needed to see that. He couldn't see it while he was looking at me."

Lil was aware of everything stopping for a moment— time, her heart. Whom had she married? She lay next to him in bed that night and on many other nights, praying that she would never do anything to make him want to teach her a lesson.

The trees were beginning to turn, but there was still a greenness and a freshness to the plants and the grass, a feeling of strength. The rich Pennsylvania soil, Gordon always said. The soil in her yard was dark and rich indeed, full of worms and shimmering with mica. She'd never done much with it—she was a city girl and knew nothing of gardening. She had lived in a big house with her parents, her sisters, and her great aunts, one of whom wore lilac water and one of whom wore rose. They kept plants in pots in all the rooms downstairs, which was her only brush with horticulture until Gordon brought her out here and she had a whole yard to fill.

Gordon had built the house himself, built it for her, he always said, although he was the one who had spoken with the architect, who had made most of the decisions. Every weekend they went out to see it while it was being built. Draft horses pulled the fieldstone blocks across the muddy lot on open wagons, their hooves sinking and squelching. Gordon consulted her on everything, but somehow it all seemed to go on without her. She knew it was her house, that she would be there long after all the workers were gone, but no matter how vividly she could picture it as she sat at her desk in their temporary apartment, writing notes or studying swatches or chips of paint, when she arrived at the sight she grew timid and walked around close to Gordon, as if always expecting to be challenged for being where she didn't belong.

She didn't feel she could lay claim to any of it, not even when Gordon walked her through the rooms that still smelled of sweet sawdust and encouraged her to be pleased with the paints she'd picked. "I chose that?" she asked over and over, as if she were being told crazy things she said in her sleep.

It all looked too big and real at first to have anything

to do with her, but eventually, with the men long gone and her own children in the airy bedrooms, she began to look with satisfaction on what she thought of as her touches. There was the pleasing mix of china pieces and books on the shelves in the living room; the copper tray filled with white pebbles on the landing that, during the winter, supported plain terra-cotta pots of geraniums, a splash of red against the vista of the gray sky and skeleton trees—like a Corot painting, she thought; the wallpaper in the library that depicted a panorama of a Chinese court, and in the hallway, a moody pattern of fox and grape against a background of purplish-gray, which she secretively always thought of as representing her perception of Gordon. He often said he liked that paper and she always smiled at his predilection for it; but she'd never quite had the nerve to let him in on her private joke, for fear of having him take it the wrong way.

Her mother had warned her not to marry a complicated man so, of course, she'd done exactly that and was rather proud of it. Not taking that piece of advice was as rebellious as she would ever be against her parents, but she liked that she had successfully gone against conventional wisdom. Her parents had grown to admire Gordon to the point of sometimes behaving as if he were their idea.

Once she hadn't been able to stop herself from reminding them that they'd been snobs at first about his background, but she was immediately sorry when they both took on the pained expressions that meant they'd seen something that offended their sensibilities—in this case, their less noble selves. The part of her that wanted to bring them to terms was no better than the part of them she sought to expose. She didn't like herself much for having done it and resolved from then on to allow them to live with their revised rendition of events, a version where they recognized Gordon's superior character and potential all along, which, in the long run, made for the more satisfying story.

Lil had had her own room in the Wynnemoor house for decades; Gordon called it her bower. They'd moved apart because he snored. He had a double bed with a canopy while she had matching wood beds with pineapple finials. She slipped her shoes off and lay down on the nearest one, being careful not to muss the spread. It was odd to be in the house without Gordon. She couldn't shake the idea that he was napping in his room just a few steps down the hall, lying curled up on his side, his silky gray hair beautiful against the pillow. The private side of their married life had ended years before, but when she stroked his brow to settle him to sleep, somehow everything that had ever been between them was there in that touch, and in his trusting response to it. She had the most profound intimacy at her fingertips.

At the shore that summer he had slept downstairs and eventually she'd moved down with him, into a bed set up on the opposite side of the dining room. Lately he'd taken to waking up in the middle of the night wanting—needing—to talk, and she sat by him while he went over and over long-ago events, as if he could still do something about them. He believed he'd made many mistakes, too many. Lil tried to argue with that, but an argument was not what he wanted. He wanted to remember. Often the sky went from dark to oyster gray to pink before he fell back to sleep. Then she would go into the kitchen and eat her breakfast in peace before the nurses arrived.

She had not wanted the nurses in the house—*her* house—but in truth, she could not manage Gordon anymore. She had tried once to help him to the commode, and there'd ended up being a mess and a shaky, humiliating afternoon for both of them. The nurse on duty, who'd been out on the back porch catching a smoke, scolded Lil, admonishing her to look at what happened when she interfered with the routine. Lil let the screen door snap behind her and had gone for a walk up on the seawall for the first time in ages, where she dared the waves to come for her until a neighbor spotted her and led her back to the house, her feet blistering in her soaked sneakers. Gordon called out to her as she walked up the stairs but she kept going, urged on by the fevered cadence of the pulse in her ears. She'd almost reached the bedroom when she heard the nurse's voice, raised to surmount Gordon's burgeoning deafness.

"Remember, Gordon, Lil has the Alzheimer's and she's not always going to act the same anymore."

"I don't want to lose her," Gordon said.

"Oh, you won't lose her. Remember what the doctor said? She has the heart of a thirty-year-old."

"I have to see that she's taken care of. She's my girl."

"We'll take care of her, Gordon, don't you worry about that. We're all right here."

Lil cringed as she thought of the way they'd touched her, followed her into the bath, taken her clothes out of the hamper, and bought her new underthings, saying her brassieres were too shot to salvage. She had tried to tell Gordon but she didn't have the words, and he didn't mind, anyway, being handled. On the contrary, he seemed to like being bathed and dressed from head to toe, as if he were a king.

She tried not to look, either, when the other women were touching him. There had been a time, right when he came home from the hospital after he broke his hip, that she had been the one to help him in the middle of the night. She felt a sharp pinch in her stomach as she remembered pulling the cold, wet sheets out from under him, the tile floor in the bathroom freezing under her feet as she stuffed the sheets in the hamper, then the sight of him inert and powerless on the bed when she returned to his room, his skin papery and pale. He had lost all the hair on his body, including his private hair.

"Damn it, Lil," he yelled when she moved him awkwardly, aggravating his wounds. Then, when he was settled again, dressed in fresh pajamas and covered to the chin with his brown blanket, he would thank her. "I don't know what I'd do without you," he said.

Lil closed her eyes and saw again the strip of exposed skin above the waist of the nurse's—Sheila's—pants. It was rosy brown and flecked with blond hair. The girl's arms spread out over and over like the beating wings of a hawk, and the band of flesh became all the skin she'd seen over the years on the beach, thousands of legs and arms and bellies and breasts. And when the girl over-came him, Gordon had laughed. It was the particular laugh that somehow expressed his essence, a combina-tion of joy with life, a boyish surprise, and an extreme cynicism. She remembered one night when one of their sons came home late after a debutante party and had gotten sick on the dining-room rug. Gordon cleaned up the whole thing by himself, then came back to bed, chuckling.

"Champagne," he said. "Remind me to tell him to stick to Scotch."

She was amazed—she thought he would have been furious that one of the children was drunk. For quite some time they'd lain awake, and he had laughed this same penetrating laugh over and over as he told tales about various drunks he had known.

She hadn't said much, as she could only view such things with a combination of disapproval and distance born of having a clear sense of what was her business and what was not, but she had observed with awe the fierce, visceral way he was alive, how much he brought to the most meager situations. There was the way he had plunged into his institutional lunch, raising his eyebrows in approval at the first taste of soup, and how warm he had been to the nurse, while seeming baffled at her devotion. Whatever else Lil felt about that display, she understood the girl's motive. It had been the driving force of Lil's life.

"Ma, are you all right?"

"Is that you, Mother?" Lil asked.

Someone sat on the bed beside her and took her by the hand. "Your mother is dead, Ma."

"She is?"

Lil opened her eyes and saw Charlotte looking at her with a small frown. It was an expression that made certain facts fall into place. "Yes, of course she is," Lil said. "I was just thinking of her."

Charlotte looked relieved. "Sometime I'm going to bring you a tape recorder, and then I'll want you to tell me everything about your life."

Lil gave a little laugh, the laugh Charlotte had once called "obfuscating." "You'll have to do that with your father. I have nothing to tell."

"I don't believe that. In many ways, I think that you're the more interesting person."

"If you think that, I'm afraid you've figured it wrong." It was an absurd idea, worthy of a laugh, obfuscating or otherwise.

"I don't think so," Charlotte murmured. "Anyway. It's nice to be here, isn't it?"

That was worthy of a laugh, too. In the house, Lil was in her life. *Nice* was not the word for it.

"It doesn't seem the same without Dad, though."

"Why can't he have the nurses here?" Lil asked.

"It costs too much. I'm sorry, Ma, but the house has to be sold."

"Sell the other one. Leave me here."

"Dad has decided. He wants you both to spend the summers at the shore and the winters in Pendleton Manor. I wish you'd try to remember all this."

In the silence that followed, they heard the man across the way calling to his wife. The voices of the children died out for a moment, then rose up again, drowning out their parents' conversation.

"How would you feel," Lil said, "if Jack did this to you."

Charlotte sprang up, her arms crossed.

"Dad isn't doing this to you. You're making this much harder than it has to be."

"Do you really expect me to live in a place like that?"

"A lot of people do. A lot of people would consider themselves lucky to be there."

"Don't talk to me as though I'm a child."

"You're behaving like one."

"Because I want to live in my own house?"

"You can't," Charlotte said. "Dad already signed the listing agreement."

"Without telling me."

"You signed it, too!"

There was a pause. Lil automatically noted the sounds of the house, the tinkling of the wind chime the grand-children had given her one Christmas, the crack of the stairs she always partly believed signaled the presence of ghosts. She pictured what it was like at night, when the sky above the pine trees was sooty and her room seemed to gather in on itself as she turned the lights out one by one.

"Go away," she said. "Leave me alone."

Charlotte began to shake. "Look, I'm exhausted. I didn't have to bring you back here at all, you know. I was trying to be nice. But this isn't my fault. You should have stood up to Dad years ago." She wiped an-grily at her eyes, flinging her tears onto the bedspread where they were absorbed into the nubbly fabric. "I hate the thought of you losing this house. You're like one of those Indian women being thrown alive onto her husband's funeral pyre. A suttee." Charlotte cried bit-terly, the way she had so many times sitting in that same spot on the bed, over so many injustices.

Lil pushed herself up and touched Charlotte's knee. "Sssh," she said. "It's all right. It's all right."

"It's not all right. It's awful." Charlotte lay her head in Lil's lap. "It's so unfair," she whispered and kept cry-ing until she was worn out. Lil marveled at her expres-siveness. Charlotte was nearly middle-aged and yet she could still cry freely. Lil pushed her hair out of the path of the tears and periodically touched a tissue to Charlotte's wet cheeks. Lil wished she could cry along with her, but she couldn't. Perhaps that was a skill she should have developed years earlier, too.

"You have the softest hands on earth," Charlotte said when she'd calmed down.

Lil looked at her. "Do I have Alzheimer's?" she asked.

"Where did you hear that?"

"The nurses."

"The nurses are idiots." Charlotte threaded her fingers through Lil's. She squeezed her hand and stood up. "I'm sorry I got so upset. I wanted to make it easier for you."

"You have. It's good you brought me back here."

Charlotte smiled awkwardly. Lil recognized her difficulty in accepting a compliment. "Anyway. I should go see what Jack's doing. Coming?"

"In a minute."

Charlotte left and Lil got up and straightened the spread. She walked around the room where she had lived the most private part of her life for nearly sixty years. It's all right, she told herself, I'll be fine. She murmured these words and others like them for some time, the litany of comfort that had sounded from her soul daily, predictably, for decades. So often she had felt the inadequacy of her formulas, their smallness in the face of real problems, but now she found some solace there, if not in the words themselves, at least in their provenance. It was a place she owned irrevocably, a perpetual retreat, the one possession she'd held back from the marriage.

She was just about ready to head downstairs when the telephone rang. Automatically she picked it up.

"Hello? Am I speaking to Mrs. Gordon Pepper?" the caller asked.

"Yes," Lil said. "This is she."

Watch the Animals

WE HAD a trying relationship with Diana Frick. She was a moneyed blue blood, the descendant of a signer, who could have been one of our old guard except that she spurned the role. Instead, she was interested in animals to the point of obsession, which in our part of the country was saying a lot. There were few among us who hadn't mourned a loyal dog or put out scraps for a stray cat or developed a smooth working relationship with a horse. Animals had a place in our lives, to be sure, and we took seriously our responsibilities toward them. But Diana went further, and always had.

For decades she'd chosen the company of other species over companionship with her own kind, a preference we naturally took as a rejection. So after she was diagnosed with lung cancer and she began to seek homes for her menagerie in the event of her death, we didn't line up at her door. Why should we? We owed her nothing. Yet the woman was fading, and we'd known her all our lives. On the telephone, in the clubs, shops, and churchyards, we tried to decide what to do.

She first came around to plead her case in autumn

when the lanes swelled with bright leaves. We couldn't help but examine her for signs of the illness, but nothing much showed; she'd always been spare. Her eyes shone blue as ever, that was the main thing. She appeared without calling first, the way we used to do when we were liable to be having tea or drinks in the afternoon and could easily accommodate company. Now we were busy but we didn't turn her away. Years of curiosity assured her a vigorous welcome.

"Let's sit outside," she said. "I've got the dogs, and I need a smoke." She noticed our raised eyebrows. "Well, I've got no reason *not* to smoke anymore, have I? I was planning to start again anyway when I turned eighty, but my schedule has been moved up a bit."

That was typical of her sense of humor—black, direct, laced with a stubbornly nonconformist aroma. We didn't smile, but she didn't care.

"Where are your bird feeders?" she asked as we walked around to the back. "It's going to get cold soon."

Her voice rasped now rather than boomed but it was still forceful.

"You put the porch furniture away already? But it's only October! Oh, all right then, we'll sit on the grass."

She always brought along at least two of her dog pack and spoke to them in a high whine to which they responded with a great deal of tongue-wagging enthusiasm. "Stop smiling!" she'd command. They'd shiver with pleasure. Often, she kissed them on their mouths.

When we were all settled and mugs of tea had been handed around she made her play.

"I'm leaving money to cover their expenses," she told us. The days were over when it was considered impolite to talk about money, but she made her offer sound like a bribe. It was yet another example of how clumsy she was with people.

"I'll need a promise in return," she continued. "I don't want to have to look up from where I'll no doubt be burning to see them shunted around. If you take them, you keep them for the duration."

We said we'd think it over, then changed the subject. When would she begin treatments, we wondered?

"Statistically my chances aren't much better with chemo and cutting than they are just twiddling my thumbs, so I'm not going to let them touch me."

She shook her head in a manner that conveyed her thorough disapproval of standard medical remedies. Good old Diana. It was a conversation stopper. We fumbled to pat the dogs.

"They're incredible, aren't they?" She grinned at our attention to them. "I've got all the dogs working as therapy animals in nursing homes. They can relate to anybody. What heart they have, considering how they were treated. We should all be more like dogs when we grow up."

When we compared notes on these visits we couldn't help but bristle. It wasn't that it was unheard of to put conditions on a request, or to shore up a good deed with

271

a financial benefit, but to do so successfully required finesse and subtlety. People want to believe they are high-minded and generous, not greedy and bought. A good monger could have offered us the same deal in terms that would have us not only clamoring to agree to it, but also feeling grateful she'd come to us.

Diana created no such feeling. The only positive we could find in her pitch was that at least she understood her animals required incentives to make them palatable. These were not purebreds, or even respectable mutts. She collected creatures that others had thrown away, the beasts left on the side of the highway or confiscated from horrific existences by her contacts at the ASPCA; the maimed sprung from labs; the exhausted retired from dog tracks; the unlucky blamed for the sins of the household and made to pay with their bodies, appetites, well-being. Immigrants from hell, she called them, and made a mission of acknowledging these crimes, beginning with naming them for their misfortunes. Thus a cat who'd been paralyzed by a motorcycle was called Harley; a dog whose leg had been chopped off by its owner earned the name Beaver Cleaver; a kitten whose eyes had been sewn shut as part of a research grant went by Kitty Wonder, and so on.

She took these animals that otherwise would have ended up euthanized at best, and she trained them and groomed them and nursed them and fed them home-cooked foods until—we had to admit—they bore a resemblance to the more fortunate of their species. They behaved, as far as we could tell. But from a practical standpoint, could they ever be considered truly trustworthy? Who knew what might set them off?

We had our children and grandchildren to consider, and guests, and pets of our own. It was not a commitment that could be made in a hurry. We told each other pretty much what we'd told her—that we'd think about it. That seemed a reasonable approach, everything considered. What else could she expect?

For a while we didn't see her much, but she became the central topic of conversation, a level of attention she'd earned several times before, usually when her books came out and we'd see or hear in interviews about her antihierarchical theories of nature, her view of animals that countered the harsh interpretations that science ascribed to their behavior, and her sorrow at the ways of the world, i.e., *our* world. She wasn't as contentious now, but we didn't believe she'd softened underneath; perhaps she was finally being a little smart, that was all. She wanted a favor, and she knew that she wasn't liable to get it if she didn't participate to some degree in normal human relations.

For the benefit of younger generations and those new to town, at dinner parties and on Sunday walks, we repeated her story—that is, how her early years had seemed to us. Her childhood didn't offer much. Her parents were jolly enough, if often absent, but so were a lot of ours. She went to Miss Dictor's, also like a lot of us,

and she rode, skated, danced. In fact, she was popular—
with the boys, naturally, because of her looks, but also
with the girls, among whom she was known as a "good
egg." Her coming-out party was of the spare-no-
expense variety and she shone even in the requisite
ivory, a hard color to wear; but she overcame it with tan
arms, the radical touch of a bracelet clasped high on
her bicep, and her thick brown hair worn long and
loose.

We assumed she'd follow the path we all walked: marriage to someone like-minded, a house of her own but
similar to her parents', children raised with the tradi-
tions that she remembered fondly, all the little habits
that connect one generation to the next. Nothing we
could see in her indicated she was headed anywhere but
in that direction. Then her brother, the heir, died in a
sailing accident, and her direction changed.

Her parents had no other children, so her father had
to face the prospect of leaving all that money, albeit in
trust, to a woman. He let it be known far and wide that
he was not happy about this. He never said a word
about losing his son, but the death of the line and his
name—his hand strayed north to massage his aching
heart when he spoke of it.

"Don't be ridiculous," we told him. "Diana will have
children, and they'll be your descendants."

"But they won't be Fricks," he said dolefully.

We felt sorry for Caroline, his wife, and could only
imagine the style of second-class citizenship in which

she must live. Our efforts to bring his thinking into the modern world made no dent, however. He died only a few years later, full of self-pity to the end. We hoped Caroline would then become a merry widow, but as often happens, she followed him shortly to the grave.

Diana got everything.

She had suitors, of course; beauty and money is an attractive combination. Every so often a fellow would say he believed he was getting somewhere with her, but it never panned out. When an interviewer later asked why she'd never married, she replied that from childhood she knew she had a vocation and couldn't afford the distraction of human love—spoken as if she were a nun. But her calling was low rather than high, down at the level of the animals, and we couldn't help but think it a delusion and a waste.

She was in her early twenties when her first book appeared, an anthropomorphic children's tale, simply yet effectively illustrated, that caught on well enough to lead to another, and more after that, until the series was a standard in every nursery, a basic christening gift. The world loved them; we alone were ambivalent. How could we not be? The characters were a barnyard of familiar types, replete with Wynnemoorian habits and belittled by suggestions of inbreeding and snobbery. We saw ourselves drawn with a harsh, loveless pen and felt stung by her portrayal—especially as we were *proud* of her.

We never spoke to her about our sense of injury, however. As we did with our own children, we showed what support we could while we waited for the day when she'd come to us offering thanks or forgiveness or perhaps a smaller token of reconciliation, a recognition in any case.

Meantime she bought a piece of land close to town and made it into a gentleman's farm, pruning the trees away until she had rolling vistas and putting in a pond and an off-limits strip of sod next to it to accommodate the nesting habits of Canadian geese. In her forties, she took in a series of foster children and brought them to the club for swims; if she thought we'd complain, we disappointed her. Instead, we offered to make calls for them to the schools, but she turned us down flat.

"I believe in public education," she scolded, as if we didn't.

We sighed and went back to waiting, although with diminishing hope.

Perhaps if she'd been average we might not have been so bothered by her hostility. Diana was marvelous, however, in exactly the way we admired most. Hers was an artless, natural beauty that managed to get by the envy of other women while arousing in the men a filial pride—a desire for her success and happiness, as well as for her. We admired her work as well; the spirit of it if not the letter. We looked at her and saw ourselves at our best. She was the sum of our efforts over the last four hundred years in this country, and back into the past to Britain and the continent, Normandy, Saxony, the high, clear springs of our culture. We wanted to be able to trot her out at our ceremonies, to have her bend her long neck to the yoke of our charities and bow before our altars, cut ribbons at our dedication ceremonies, and stand side by side with us at our weddings and confirmations and graduations.

That she cared so little about those kinds of gatherings was irksome to say the least. People scrabbled all their lives for just a fraction of what was hers from the start, yet she didn't feel fortunate or grateful or privileged. She preferred to be in her barn prying stones out of her horses' hooves or sitting motionless by a closet door watching a new litter of kittens pump blindly at their mother. Those things were fine, in moderation. It was her excess that we didn't understand. Or maybe it was the opposite; we understood it all too well and were afraid of it.

We'd taken to heart the often repeated caveat from our childhoods that the elders applied to all manner of deviance—*think what would happen if everyone behaved like that!* The consequence was never exactly specified; for most of us, the implication of chaos and breakdown was enough. We knew our own bad thoughts, after all, knew what we had to suppress. We understood why we couldn't indulge our baser natures or the full range of our whims; we might lose what we had if we did. How had it happened that Diana didn't understand what was at stake?

The final straw came when she published her autobiography. At last we learned her gripes about us, and they cast a wide net. She recounted various instances of

cruelty she'd observed as a child, among which were in-
cidents that had bothered us, too. None of us had ap-
plauded Harold Johnson's shooting of his dog for eating
the Thanksgiving turkey, nor were we amused when
someone nailed a cat through its feet to a plank of
wood. Yet did she extend us any credit for empathy and
shock? No. We were a town without pity, a callous
bunch who didn't realize, as she did, that animals had
feelings and souls. Would we get rid of one of our children for taking a long time to be toilet trained or shed-
ding too much? Would we call the police on a stranger
for asking directions? Yet we perpetrated these evil
deeds on animals without thinking twice.

Her arguments were silly, but the book became a hit.
Souls, she claimed. That was the crux of what she had
to tell the world. As always, she pushed it beyond the
beyond.

The next foray in her campaign consisted of a mailing,
eight double-sided pages of pictures and descriptions of
her menagerie. The cover page sported the title "full
disclosure," and as usual, Diana meant what she said.
She was certainly no mistress of persuasion—we already knew that. Yet these pages set a new standard in
their complete refusal to make even the smallest nod to
the principles of salesmanship. Beneath a grainy picture
of each animal she described their routines in detail—
ear cleanings, pillings, and other noxious chores—as
well as offering predictions as to what health problems

they were likely to suffer in the future. Then there were their habits and eccentricities: this one had to drink from the tap in the kitchen, that one slept under the covers by Diana's knees, and on and on. For the armchair behaviorists among us, the document offered interesting anecdotal evidence of how creatures adapt to hardship and abuse/luxury and pampering—not to mention what it revealed about Diana. No wonder she never went out!

After receiving these pages we called to ask how she was.

"Not bad, with the minor complication of stage four lung cancer," she replied.

Wasn't she doing anything at all?

"I'm killing the pain. Of course, they're queer about that, never want to give you enough. What difference does it make if you become addicted to opiates when you're riddled with the big *C?* I have my sources, though. Veterinary drugs are easy to come by."

We told her we knew lots of doctors and had ins at the university hospital if she'd like us to make a few calls. She responded by lecturing us on birds and their need of water in the winter; we could buy solar birdbaths from such-and-such catalogs.

"So no decision yet?" she prompted.

Not yet, we replied.

"Don't wait too long, or I won't be around to hear it. But no pressure!"

Ha ha ha.

. . .

Then she surprised us. We were at church for the children's choir service on Christmas Eve afternoon and were settling ourselves to the tune of the organist's prelude when Diana walked in and took a place on the aisle two-thirds of the way back. For the next few moments the old cavernous nave rippled with elbowings and turnings around and head tiltings; immediately we began to compose comments for later about how she was the second-to-last person we expected to see there, as the old joke went—the last being Jesus. The organist struck the chord for the processional, but we took a beat longer to stand than was customary as we watched her kneel all the way to the ground to say her private prayer.

How beautiful she was, the picture of devotion, like Jennifer Jones in *The Song of Bernadette*. Then we stood and she disappeared beneath taller heads as the children came up the aisle clad in the garb of the ancient Israelites à la Italian medieval painting: drapes, drapes, drapes. They made faces and batted at the frankincense that one of the kings swung dramatically in a censer, and we gave them the usual pleased, encouraging smiles as they passed.

We loved them best, better than anything, but at that moment we were grateful when they were finally all up front posed in the familiar tableau so we could gawk at Diana. It appeared that she'd bought a new suit for the occasion; we hadn't seen her legs in years. She participated fully in the service and afterward joined the crowd in the vestry who were waiting for children and grandchildren to drop backstage the raiments and constraints of their holy personae. We assumed she wanted to congratulate them on their performances, to play the village eccentric by speaking to them exclusively, but she turned quite amiably to us.

"Such wonderful music," she said.

"We have a new organist," we informed her—although in fact he may have been well down the line since she was last there.

"Lovely," she said. Then the children appeared and loudly gave their insiders' versions of the pageant. Diana was lost in the mayhem as we walked outside.

Dark had fallen by then, but the day was strangely balmy; there was a low moon in the purple sky. It wasn't the Currier & Ives Christmas we all held as the ideal but it was Christmas nonetheless. Our church was built of fieldstone. In the precincts of the churchyard, we may as well have been in the Home Counties. Even the graveyard did not betray us; the dates went back far enough to afford us a claim to a history and a past. We knew that teenagers sometimes went there at night to try to spook themselves—but that seemed an impulse the flipside of Sunday morning and the rector ignored them as long as they did no harm.

Many of us took a detour before going to our cars and walked for a few moments down the narrow pathways among the markers. Here were our parents, grandparents, ancestors. In spite of our tacit assumption that the here and now was the end of it, we found ourselves addressing them in our minds. "It's Christmas Eve again," we informed them, "and, as always, everything and nothing has changed." We didn't go in much for putting flowers on the graves but it was seemly to stop for a moment of acknowledgment. It was an interlude of calm before the revels, part of our yearly ritual.

Then Diana walked past us and made her way to the Frick family plot. We saw her bow her head, and her hands raise to her face. We winced. We'd all had the thought when standing by those graves that we'd be there soon enough ourselves, but for Diana the time was imminent. She wasn't toying with history as we were, but staring directly at her own extinction. It was natural, yes, but still awful. When she rejoined us we could see the disease in her. Without benefit of the flattering church light she appeared emaciated, her skin thin and gray.

"We're having cocktails at the Gardners'. Why don't you come?" We didn't like the idea of her going home to an empty house. Not on Christmas. Even by choice.

She smelled like our adolescent girls who put vanilla on their pulse points in the summer.

"I thank you very much," she said, "but I have mouths to feed."

She said this plainly, imbuing it with no hint. Yet the spirit of the day was in us, and the favor she'd asked seemed logical rather than an imposing chore.

Laddie Phillips spoke first. "Look," he said. "I'll take that greyhound. Rescued from a dog track, was he?"

Mina Jones, never one to be outdone, instantly said she'd take two cats—*at least*, she added, affording her room to maneuver in case anyone displayed a more impressive generosity.

Ben Knowlton, home from college, asked for the pit bull.

"The Staffordshire terrier," Diana instructed. Then, as if coaching herself to be agreeable, she gave a shake of her head that ended in a softening of her expression. "But perhaps it's a good thing to say pit bull. You and she can be ambassadors for the breed."

And so it went until nearly every animal was spoken for, and promises made to find placements for the rest.

"So how about that drink?" we offered again.

There was a pause. How could she refuse? She couldn't, and finally, she understood that. She followed us out of the parking lot.

The next morning, after the presents had all been opened and the wrapping paper was blazing in the fireplace, we felt the usual letdown, not the smallest part of which was a bout of regret for acting so impulsively with Diana. By lunchtime, however, we felt ourselves again and glad of our gesture. We'd opened a door that had been locked for decades. It seemed a good omen for the new year.

After that, we began calling to ask how she was. Soon, without calling first, we stopped by to drop off leftovers. We offered to take her dogs for a walk so she didn't have to go out in the rain. In other words, we did all in our power to show her that even if she had never taken our side, we were nevertheless on hers.

At first, predictably, she declined, and when we wouldn't hear of it, she flat-out refused our ministrations.

"Go away," she'd shout when we knocked on her windows. It was quite a picture seeing this frail shrinking creature waving her bird arms at us, as if she could keep us out. We no longer took it personally. She was dying and there was no time to dwell on slights or insults, no room for the luxuries of holding grudges and taking offense. She needed us at last, and her need was as good as an apology. We took her keys to the hardware store and made copies, then set up a schedule of rotating shifts so that except for at night after we'd tucked her into bed, she was never alone. It was a lot of work, but it was what we'd do for any sister or mother or aunt; it was simply right.

The one difficulty was her habit of sleeping with all her dogs arrayed around the room. We didn't think it was safe; if any one of them knocked her over, her bones would surely shatter. Before we left we put them in their cages, but when we arrived the next morning there they were, on her bed and all along the walls like wainscoting. No matter how patiently we explained the danger to her, she persisted in sneaking downstairs at night and letting them up.

"We're going to have to put you in a nursing home if you don't take care of yourself," we told her. We said it out of exasperation, the way we told the children that Santa wouldn't come if they were bad.

"Dogs go off on their own to die," she said.

"You're not a dog." It was like talking to a child, and we became childish ourselves, doing it. We wanted to wring her skinny neck.

"Leave me alone," she said.

We were tempted, but we couldn't. She had no one else.

One early spring morning the house seemed unnaturally quiet. Usually Diana had let the dogs out by the time we arrived. It was the one part of her old routine she maintained even after she'd become too weak to manage their heavy bowls of food and water anymore. In our experience, she'd never kept them waiting past seven. And so we knew.

We weren't squeamish, yet we tiptoed up the stairs and approached her room with trepidation. We needn't have worried, though. The scene, when we finally faced it, was peaceful. Diana had that mythic look of death that apes sleep while the absence of her singular spirit made the room feel empty. The only disturbing note was that the dogs were still with her—the large ones in their customary spots along the walls, and the smaller creatures arrayed around her on the bed like a wreath. When we entered, they eyed us lugubriously.

"Out!" we commanded, but they didn't move.

Then we forgot them for some time as we began to piece together details we'd overlooked at first glance. We pulled the curtains and, in the early light, saw that a crust of powder ringed her lips, and scattered on the bedside table and the floor below lay dozens of gelatin capsules, all of them opened and empty. How typical of Diana to do things her way, regardless of any constraints of law or ethics. Yet we didn't disapprove of her for it. It was her choice, we decided, as we would want it to be for ourselves. There was no reason for anyone else to know, however. The world at large isn't always as understanding as one's own kind, and we feared they might judge her weak or criminal. We cleaned up the pill bottles, washed out the glass, and tucked the note she'd left in a pocket for disposal at home. She hadn't written much anyway, just three words: *watch the dogs*. It was an odd exhortation as we'd already agreed to it. It reminded us, though, that they were still in the room.

"Shoo!" we ordered, with no luck. Then someone recalled the ironic command Diana used when she wanted them to hop in their crates. It might at least get them downstairs, where we could deal with them more easily.

"Prison time!" we said, imitating her singsong way of speaking to them. The phrase got *some* results; they stood and walked to the door. Then they stopped, though, and simply stared. Was there another command we should be giving? We racked our brains. Meanwhile, it was eerie how they looked at us. It was as if they understood they'd never see her again, and that within the day they'd be in strange houses, separated from each other, adjusting to new circumstances and people and demands.

"Prison time!" we said again.

This time they seemed ready to obey, but not before taking what appeared to be a last look back at Diana. Was it possible they had an inkling of what was happening? No doubt they recognized death; but the idea that they might feel *grief* was another matter. That was a notion from Diana's realm, not ours. We'd interpret the dogs' baleful behavior as consternation at a disruption in their routine. Diana would say they were bereft. Who was right? It occurred to us that the greatest tribute we could pay her would be to give her, for once, the benefit of the doubt. (Perhaps the only tribute—she'd always said she wouldn't be caught dead having a funeral.) And why not? What could we lose by extending them our empathy; what would we gain by holding back? We afforded them a moment of silence. What went on during that time we would never know. The way they looked at us afterward, though: we didn't believe in an afterlife, not a corporeal one at least, but in spite of ourselves, we hoped she could see.

Finally we coaxed them outside and began to notify everyone. The man at *The New York Times* had a file on Diana already and rang back to verify the details.

"Name of hospital?" he asked.

Oh no, we said, no hospital, none of that. On the contrary, the end was quite soulful, what we'd all like when the time comes—to die at home, during sleep, surrounded by friends.